SEARCHING
for the
EMPEROR

Roberto Pazzi

Translated by M. J. Fitzgerald

SEARCHING
for the
EMPEROR

The story of a Russian regiment
lost in Siberia during the Revolution,
in search of the imprisoned Tsar

Alfred A. Knopf   New York   1988

THIS IS A BORZOI BOOK
PUBLISHED BY ALFRED A. KNOPF, INC.
Copyright © 1988 by Maria Fitzgerald
All rights reserved under International and Pan-American Copy-
right Conventions. Published in the United States by Alfred A. Knopf,
Inc., New York. Distributed by Random House, Inc., New York.

Originally published in Italy as *Cercando L'Imperatore*
by Casa Editrice Marietti S.p.A., Casale Monferatto
Copyright © 1985 by Casa Editrice Marietti, Sp.A.
This translation was originally published in Great Britain by André
Deutsch Limited, London

Library of Congress Cataloging-in-Publication Data
Pazzi, Roberto [*date*]
Searching for the emperor.
Translation of: Cercando l'imperatore.
I. Title.
PQ4876.A98C413   1988   853'.914   88–45220
ISBN 0–394–55998–3

Manufactured in the United States of America
First American Edition

TO E
because without her
I would not have been able to
search for the Emperor

SEARCHING
for the
EMPEROR

1

The telegraph had not worked for months now. The governor of Vachitino, Ivan Alexandrovich, had planned a sortie that February to break through to Tobolsk, but then changed his mind. The last items of news the summer before spoke of great changes that had taken place in St. Petersburg—no one in Vachitino called the capital by its new name Petrograd—that some units of the army had mutinied but the authority of the Tsar had been reestablished. Someone had even said that the Tsar himself was in Tobolsk, but no one believed this—it was too absurd:

—These people don't know what they're saying. The Tsar in Tobolsk ... nonsense,— Ivan Alexandrovich muttered, shrugging his shoulders.

Vachitino was so far away that Tatar merchants who set out in spring to reach it always made a will. The governor had all the time in the world to quarrel with his wife Tania, especially since his duties no longer required him to check up on the river folk, who had disappeared after fighting against the cold and losing their particular war.

Once upon a time the land had not been so icy, it had

yielded abundant food and, like so many other parts of Siberia, in winter one could live from the stores of food harvested
in summer. Now all the land along the river was frozen, and
Ivan Alexandrovich would come by on his sled, flanked by his
guards, and the inhabitants of Vachitino stripped the abandoned houses for firewood. It didn't take much to predict that
at this rate Vachitino itself would be swallowed up by the ice,
but anyone who tried to say as much was taken for an idiot.
The governor continued to imagine a peaceful flow of years,
with nothing in the future to prevent him from dying of old
age like all his predecessors and from following them, accompanied by the priest and the entire town, to the cemetery
behind the apse of the church, where they all slept next to
their wives.

Every once in a while the telegraph worried Ivan Alexandrovich: it had been silent for months now.

—What's going on in Tobolsk? Don't they realize it's broken? Can they really leave us like this all winter?—

—What could they possibly have to tell us? You'll see, it'll
be repaired next summer, and you can go and check your poles
one by one.—

Tania invariably found some reason to disagree with her
husband. On Sundays, Ivan Alexandrovich went to Mass in
full uniform, stood by his wife in her plumed hat and personally intoned the hymn in honor of the Tsar and the Tsaritsa.
Every day he went by the fort, one of the new brick buildings,
and dropped in on the commanding officer.

—No change, Your Excellency. All present and correct.—

The twenty deportees in question were as much part of the
town as the druggist, the priest, the governor's wife, the

plumes in her hat and the chickens in her yard; all were there because it was their destiny to be there.

The greatest event in Vachitino was the spring market, but no market had ever caused such a ferment as the arrival of the Preobrazhenskii Regiment, the morning it entered the town from the south, on the side by the river. Nadezhda, the washerwoman's idiot daughter, sounded the alarm, rushing from one end of town to the other like a squirrel:

—Soldiers, soldiers, there are soldiers, here, soldiers!—

—What soldiers, Nadezhda, you're dreaming, what soldiers?—

—No, no, she's right, look down there, she's right!—

The soldiers were moving forward, preceded by dispatch runners looking for the governor, long columns of men marching with field artillery, wagons, horses, standard-bearers. Never-ending columns marching in step to a heavy regular beat, marching with ashen, expressionless faces, as if they had come from a country where everything that could be seen had been. They looked as if they couldn't see the guards, the children, the peasants, the women, the Jewish shopkeepers, the priest, the officer of the fort, the governor, who had all crowded together to watch.

The officer in command was a colonel, Prince Ypsilanti; on horseback he looked just like the statue of Saint George in the church.

—Look, look at the pipes, the trumpets and drums!— The sons of Jonas the Jewish wine seller had pushed themselves to the front until they were almost under the carts, and discovered the band. Despite their exhaustion, the soldiers marched in step to their band, following the prince's order, given as soon as he had picked out through his field glasses the domed bell-tower above the snow:

—Major, halt the columns. Have the men fall in in marching order. We will enter to the beat of the drums!— Then he adjusted the white silk scarf around his neck as if they were entering Petrograd under the Alexander arch, before the Emperor.

It was he, always he, with his disdainful gestures, closed in a silence that allowed no familiarity. And yet he shared in his men's labors, shared their experience of the terrible aimless march, living through it day by day since they had lost all contact with the Supreme Command.

Grand Duke Nicholas had made the proposal during the last meeting of the General Staff at Mogilev, in the presence of the Tsar:

—Your Imperial Majesty, the Preobrazhenskii Regiment does not belong here; it's made up of soldiers who've always proved their worth against the Turks, ever since the Crimean War. I suggest posting them down there, on the Eastern Front,— and the Tsar had agreed. At the moment of putting his signature on the order, Nicholas II had paused, with the pen still raised:

—The Tsarevich will be your honorary colonel.—

—It is a privilege the regiment hopes to continue to deserve, Your Imperial Majesty,— the chief of staff had replied, springing to attention.

So the regiment had moved from Galicia to the Caspian Sea along internal routes, and when the revolution broke out, the troops had already been immobilized for two months by the Russian winter.

The colonel in command of the regiment, a childhood

friend of Grand Duke Nicholas, had tried to block the transfer; he did not like that Asian tradition: the reputation for
military affinity with the Turks was contrary to the purely
Western idea of national glory fostered in him by a Parisian
education during the last years of Napoleon III's reign. He
wanted to fight in Prussia and Pomerania against the Germans. His mother, a Greek princess, daughter of the marquis
of Santorino, had imbued him with a Greek hatred and scorn
for the Turks. Well. Someone had been out to please him:
they had not run across any Turks and the regiment had
moved north in search of the enemy that was retreating from
another front, routed by the English.

One Sunday in March 1917 during Mass, just at the moment of the consecration, Prince Ypsilanti heard shouts from
the camp:

—Colonel, I want to know at once what's going on,— he
had whispered to one of his battalion commanders.

A group of Jews crossing the steppes had told of great
upheavals in St. Petersburg.

—And the Tsar?— the soldiers asked.

—He's at the front, no one knows for sure, they say he's
abdicated. . . .— It was impossible, of course, but the prince
worried: he would have liked to talk to those Jews himself, to
give those filthy people a taste of Russian authority, but they
had vanished as if they had never existed.

—Could the soldiers have dreamt them up?— Captain
Karel had asked, reporting back to the colonel.

From that day a kind of fever spread through the regiment,
a fever that kept many tossing through the nights, those long
winter nights identical to the dark mornings, with the soldiers
huddled in their tents waiting for the return of spring. Winter

was one long night here, and it was years since anyone had seen so much snow, not even the terrible winter of the war against Japan; and these were territories no one seemed ever to have seen before; no one knew where they were, they only knew they had left the last town behind in November.

Could one keep an entire regiment in midair like this, with no orders? The colonel toyed with the idea of sending a company west, toward the Urals, but then resolved to move with the whole regiment. He had to reestablish contact with the General Staff, and he wanted to return to the Western Front.

The strange news from the Jews had meanwhile spread throughout the regiment, and every day some detail was added. It seemed as if the Jews had talked about it day and night nonstop: the Tsar had abdicated at the front, the Tsaritsa and the family were prisoners in the palace; even the most faithful regiments in the capital had embraced the revolutionaries. Some even said that a republic had been declared. The suspense could not go on: solid news, action, were needed. But what? That was the start of the march which was to continue for almost a full year.

—Inform the troops that we're heading for a secret destination of fundamental strategic importance. We must take advantage of their loyalty, their sense of honor, and put an end to these absurd rumors once and for all. Gentlemen, I'm relying on you. We will try to reach the nearest center where we can telegraph Petrograd. It's true, the season is not on our side, but we cannot stay still and wait. War is war and we are soldiers; there is fighting going on and it's going on without us; the Tsar is having to do without his Preobrazhenskii; that cannot go on, nor can we stay here without further orders.

Remember the oath of allegiance that binds us until death to the sacred person of the Emperor. Any questions, gentlemen?—

—A question, sir. If we strike camp at this time of year, won't we stand to lose a lot of men without engaging combat?— It was the commander of the Second Battalion, a man who seldom spoke.

—There are various ways of fighting,— Prince Ypsilanti replied. —Personally I consider facing death to obey the Emperor's orders more glorious than fighting the Turks. Any more questions? Good. Chief of staff will attend for final details. We are leaving at three this afternoon. God save the Tsar!—

—God save the Tsar!— the officers had echoed. And at three o'clock the march began. For a long time the men were convinced they were heading for the Urals, on their way back to Europe, but gradually as they trudged, rivers, mountains and lakes seemed to disappear from the map, leaving behind large white sheets of ice and snow.

—Where does that man want to drag us to? You don't march in winter,— was the general grumble. The medical officers began to record the first cases of frostbite, the first limb amputations, finally the first deaths. At the daily briefing the unit commanders reported on the growing rebelliousness among the rank and file:

—It's not so much the marching itself, sir, as not knowing where they're heading. For example, yesterday my orderly had a word with the corporal in one company–there was talk of a whole platoon deserting.—

—Deserting? At this point? Surely that's just talk?—

—Sir, provisions are running out, and the quartermaster's men are not dumb. And then there are the horses: we've had to shoot more than fifty since the outbreak of the epidemic, and they can't even be eaten.—

But desertion? Where in heaven's name would they go? thought the prince.

—Gentlemen, I want the strictest discipline, absolute obedience; shoot deserters and agitators if you have to. Stick to the letter of the law. Remember we are at war.—

The winter of 1917 had passed this way, amid constant losses. The few villages they came across in their march had no more information about what was happening at the front and in the capital to pass on to the prince; any plans of desertion had evaporated in the vast expanse of snow and ice; supplies continued to dwindle, men and horses to die of the cold.

Finally summer had come and the survivors had made provisions of food, fodder and horses; the prince had been able to reorganize the regiment and to hope that the day of return was not far. The march had continued into the following winter, right up to the time when the telegraph poles of Vachitino had been spotted. The prince had calculated that a two-day march would bring them to a place with a telegraph station.

By the time the order to halt was given, Governor Ivan Alexandrovich already stood in front of the prince:

—It is my great honor to welcome you to Vachitino, Colonel. I am Ivan Alexandrovich Tjagunov, the governor.—

The prince dismounted from his horse.

—Prince Alexander Ilarionovich Ypsilanti. I am greatly honored, madam.— Tania blushed with excitement when he bowed and kissed her hand. The people meanwhile were crowding around the soldiers. Some were offering food and drink, some were eagerly asking news, but there were some who showed little enthusiasm.

—Well, now we'll lose the little we have, look at them, they're dying of hunger, this is all we need.—

—Look, look at the horses, they're sick, they'll give their disease to ours, look, they can barely stand.—

—Heaven help and preserve us from these people if they stay.—

—And the war? Have we beaten the Germans yet?—

—Have we entered Berlin yet?—

—But where do you come from? What regiment is this?—

Later Ivan Alexandrovich and Tania were introduced to all the other officers in the governor's office, under the big portrait of the Tsar and the Tsaritsa. The governor had been quick to invite the whole regimental headquarters staff to lunch and Tania had rushed to the kitchens:

—Prince Ypsilanti, Prince Ypsilanti at lunch in my house, Prince Ypsilanti, a friend of the Tsar.— Swinging between happiness and dismay, she busied herself alongside the kitchen maid to ensure her guests would be comfortable, while the colonel informed the governor of the regiment's needs.

It was wartime and the governor knew well that the need for horses, fodder, food and clothes must not be neglected, under pain of requisition. That blasted telegraph, he was thinking. If only I could have asked for instructions. Why did the Preobrazhenskii Regiment have to fall to me of all people; why did it have to land here at Vachitino, of all the places there are in Siberia? Prince Ypsilanti then asked if he could get in touch immediately with Petrograd.

—How, sir? There is no telegraph.—

—You are joking, Governor. What about those poles that run parallel to the road on which we came? Did I dream them?—

—NO, no, Your Excellency, the poles are there all right. But the line has been interrupted for months now, and the failure is not in our province. I can't see that it will be repaired until summer now, I'm afraid.—

A deep silence descended in the reception hall of the governor of Vachitino, a silence so deep, the worms could be heard gnawing in the cupboard crammed with the documents of the previous governors. The twenty officers were turned to stone. Ivan Alexandrovich was fearful for a minute, looking at those living statues: it was as if the death of the Tsar had been announced. What did it matter if the telegraph wasn't working? Well, it hadn't worked for months and they hadn't died, had they? Everything was the same, the Tsar was there, in St. Petersburg, the governor was here, winter was winter, summer was on the way, the exiles were behaving themselves, the chickens were laying large eggs, Boris's eldest daughter had borne triplets. What on earth could be missing? What need was there for a telegraph line?

Prince Ypsilanti stared out of the window at the isbas half-hidden by snow, twisting and untwisting his hands held behind his back, thinking: Then the devil has brought me here. Why Vachitino? Why must a blind man meet only another blind man? This is the other half of me, this town, that's all it is, my other half. It was waiting and I've come after a year, come all this way to prepare the thousand men left of the two thousand I had in my charge, to prepare them for their death, death caused by a broken thread. Because we are either the death of this town, or it is our death. . . . He turned slowly and looking at a point above their heads, he addressed his officers:

—Gentlemen, I have decided. We march again in two weeks. The Tsar cannot do without his Preobrazhenskii. We will enter Europe, heading west, toward the Urals. If we are lucky we will find a town where the telegraph works.— He lowered his gaze toward Ivan Alexandrovich. The fellow's mad, the governor thought. It's a blessing for us to have them off our hands, but I'll be going to certain death.

Old Khabalov, commander of the First Battalion, broke the silence:

—What was the last news from Petrograd, Your Excellency, before the telegraph line was interrupted?—

—Some rioting immediately quelled and rumors that the Tsar is in Siberia, in Tobolsk even. It's nonsense. . . .—

Prince Ypsilanti lifted his head abruptly.

—What did you say? The Tsar in Tobolsk?—

—Yes, Prince, that was one of the last messages of the summer. It was one of the most confusing, the line was already failing. But I know it's impossible, I merely mention it to keep you informed,— Ivan Alexandrovich answered.

—And how do you know what is and what is not possible to our Lord the Tsar? What makes you think that His Imperial Majesty would want to exclude this region from his care? Barely a year ago at breakfast with the Emperor on the feast day of our regiment, His Majesty deigned to tell me that he would like to visit this region of Siberia and that he planned to push beyond the Urals after an inspection of the Eastern Front. He's certainly there, at Tobolsk, where the telegraph said he was. And, gentlemen, he needs us. Forgive me, Governor, if I confer with my officers here in your house. Perhaps you could join us again in a few minutes.—

After Ivan Alexandrovich had left the room, Ypsilanti turned to his officers:

—Gentlemen, we are here and the Tsar is in Tobolsk where he is undoubtedly waiting for us: this is what the troops must know, what the telegraph has told us. The Tsar's orders are clear, to reach him as soon as possible and return to Petrograd with him. The Preobrazhenskii Regiment, founded by Peter the Great, is the Tsar's sword, and the Tsar needs it to restore order in the capital. Do I make myself clear?—

The officers understood what he wanted to do.

—But if some of the soldiers have already heard that the telegraph line is broken, how will they believe us?—

—Very simple. We have engineers and telegraphers; we will put them to work and pretend to restore the line. It will be an operation during which three men I shall choose will die in an explosion to break up a mass of ice. The governor will keep quiet, he wants us out of here. Three lives will save hundreds. The soldiers will believe me.—

The officers looked at the man with a certain embarrassment, but also with admiration: there could be no objection; they could not stay in Vachitino, the provisions could not feed the inhabitants and the regiment. There must be some truth in those rumors of sedition and difficulty for the Tsar, seeing as they corresponded to what the Jews had said. They might as well tell the rank and file that the Tsar was at Tobolsk and needed them, to encourage them to resume their march, to rely yet again on their strong loyalty. To stay behind meant death by starvation for all; to go meant there was at least a chance of making it, even at the cost of human lives. It was necessary to tell a lie and leave.

Ivan Alexandrovich was called in and informed of the decision. Everything happened exactly as Prince Ypsilanti had hoped: the engineer and two telegraphers officially repaired the telegraph line, then died in an explosion; the inhabitants, happy to get rid of those who, had they stayed, would have eaten them out of house and home, opened their hearts and homes exuberantly to six days of festivities that cost many the wine and vodka of years. Even though half of Vachitino's cured meat went into the regiment's provisions, the governor was satisfied; at least he had salvaged his fodder and some of the medicines, as well as whatever he had managed to hide.

As soon as word got around that the telegraph was working, a throng gathered outside the post office, but they found a large notice posted on the door, signed by Ivan Alexandrovich: THE TELEGRAPH OFFICE IS REQUISITIONED BY THE PREOBRAZHENSKII REGIMENT UNTIL THE 30TH. Some had immediately protested, but by the next day everything was quiet at the little yellow building, and the guard was already wondering why on earth he should be there, in front of that notice in which no one was interested, stamping his feet against the cold.

Tobolsk was far but not that far, not on the other side of the world; during the good season it could be reached in a few weeks, but Ivan Alexandrovich could not calculate how long it would take in winter through all the snow. When Tania learned from her husband that the regiment was leaving, headed for Tobolsk, she made the sign of the cross:

—Sweet Virgin of Kazan, they're crazy; Ivan Alexandrovich you must not let those poor Christian souls leave.— But for once her husband convinced her that it was for the good of all that they go. Prince Ypsilanti mustered and talked to his soldiers, battalion by battalion, and did not even need to make long speeches: the news that the Tsar was at Tobolsk and that he had given them orders to join him there had the desired effect on the troops who were a little restored by the pause.

—The Tsar will reenter Petrograd at the head of the Preobrazhenskii— were the last words of the prince to his decimated battalions, and he had not managed to finish before his words were drowned by the roar:

—To Petrograd, to Petrograd. Long live the Tsar!—

The day before departure, the chief of staff looked for the prince while he was inspecting the armory.

—Forgive the interruption, sir, but there's a man here who's been waiting since this morning to speak to you.—

—Who is he?—

—The shoemaker, sir; he's been waiting for hours in front of headquarters, and he won't budge until he's talked to you, Your Excellency.—

It was Boris the shoemaker. He'd come to ask to join the regiment; he could not stay behind mending shoes for the people of Vachitino while the Tsar was gathering his loyal people to recapture St. Petersburg:

—What do you mean? The Tsar is in full possession of his Imperial powers, he needs no one. Whoever told you otherwise?—

Old Boris didn't want them to think him too stupid not to see that something grave was afoot there, at Tobolsk, and he begged and implored the colonel to take him with them, to fight in the regiment; he could fight, he had fought against the

Turks as a boy, he had been wounded in the war against Japan. The prince had to make use of the full reasonableness of his authority to reassure Boris, giving him fulsome details of his last visit to Tsarskoe Selo, telling him of the Grand Duchess Anastasia's watercolors, Maria's probable wedding, the jewels offered for Russia's victory by the devout Tsaritsa to the Virgin of Vladimir, the miraculous icon that had stopped Tamerlane in his tracks.

—And the heir, the heir to the throne?— Boris insisted eagerly.

When the chief of staff came in to bring the next day's orders for the colonel's signature, he found Boris the shoemaker and Prince Ypsilanti quietly seated in headquarters, smoking cigars, talking of the Imperial family as if they had just left it a minute before at the palace, discussing, as old faithful friends can, the severity with which the Tsar handled Olga and Tatiana, the two eldest daughters, and the indulgence of the Tsaritsa toward Aleksei:

—She'll end up spoiling him too much, that boy. . . .— And so the prince succeeded in taking leave of Boris with the promise that as soon as they reentered Petrograd an invitation would be telegraphed for the shoemaker to join them at the palace.

—Major, it is men like Boris the shoemaker who make the empire what it is,— Ypsilanti told his chief of staff, who was astonished by the forbearance of the prince who was usually so reserved.

Boris the shoemaker returned home reassured and gave permission for his daughters to go and say good-bye to the soldiers, thinking of Olga and Tatiana who had so little freedom to enjoy their youth. The Tsar must understand that youth is youth, he thought, hammering nails into the soles of the boots of Grigori, the Tatar butcher.

The Preobrazhenskii Regiment started its march toward Tobolsk on the last Sunday in February, and during the months that followed, Boris had never been so cheerful: his wife Anna noticed that after dinner he disappeared back into the shop and she could hear him hammering and singing until late. At that hour, after a day's work, what could he possibly be doing locked in the shop? When she asked him, Boris smiled mysteriously:

—You'll see, you'll see.—

One evening in April he called her to the shop and showed her the most beautiful pair of boots that ever a shoemaker had made: they were white, edged in soft red leather, with dark large nails and silver spurs. Boris had copied them from a picture of a mounted king in a book that belonged to his youngest son Andrei.

—Andrei, read what is written there,— he had said, pointing at the caption under the picture. And the child had spelled out:

—Na-po-le-on at Wa-ter-loo.—

Anna was stunned at the sight of the boots.

—Boris, did you make them? Was it you, really? But who on earth could wear them?—

—Yes, I made them. They're for the Tsar.—

The next day the telegraph began working again and the post office clerk read the message on the flimsy blue strips of paper: TSAR PRISONER TOBOLSK. STOP. SOVIET REPUBLIC GREETS COMRADES VACHITINO. STOP. SIGNED. TOBOLSK SO-VIET. STOP.

2

The Whites had been shelling the town for days, and the noise was getting nearer by the hour: the constant crackling of shots was enough to drive crazy those who could not move. Kharitonov only knew that along the river near the cathedral two houses had been gutted. It was intolerable only to be able to gather snippets of information from what Dimitri the soldier let slip to the cook in exchange for choice morsels of food. On that airless July evening, when one was not allowed to open a window, it really was impossible. The heavy regular step of the guards resounded below, an unpleasant smell of beans came from the kitchen, and from the anteroom the scent of a soldier's pipe. Dimitri kept on glancing more than tenderly at Maria; he was embarrassed to be among the jailers of the Imperial family, imprisoned at Ekaterinburg in the requisitioned house of the engineer Ipatiev; they had been brought here from house arrest in Tobolsk on April 30.

How wonderful it would be to be still in Tobolsk, where everyone was so kind, where people vied with each other to bring them all sorts of good things. . . . Sometimes the guards had had to fetch them in before their daily exercise hour was up because of the crowds that thronged to kiss the Tsar's hand. Yes, at Tobolsk they'd been all right; they had almost not noticed that they were prisoners in a lost corner of Siberia. Time had stood still in the sleepy town full of enclosed orders, whose blind and decrepit Bishop Hermogenes continued to receive letters from the Empress Mother instigating him to head a counterrevolution, to emulate Saint Hermogenes, the enemy of the Tatars. Poor Maman, imagine if she were here now, here at Ekaterinburg, to witness how the Tsar and the Tsaritsa of all the Russias were being treated ... much better that she should be over there, in her beloved Crimea, from where she could flee on an English ship. And lucky too that his brother George had died when the dynasty was in its full splendor, back in 1899, having refused to take a step into the century his brothers had had to enter. He, Nicholas, had no illusions left; he felt that Russia, the authentic, the tormented Russia had been reabsorbed into its most deeply buried roots, as it had under the Tatars. His land was gathering up its sap, building up strength for a distant future that excluded him, and his own sacrifice was part of the plan. No White regiment would reach and save them: they were shades already, Siberian ghosts. It was over. He remembered the moment the train had drawn into Pskov station the morning of March 1, 1917. There had been no guard of honor, and only General Ruzsky waiting for him on the platform with his second-in-command. They had been the ones to announce to the Tsar the defection of the Petrograd and Tsarskoe Selo garrisons, and of the guards and the cossacks of the Imperial escort. He had not anticipated such a complete and such a swift collapse, not even when he had allowed himself to daydream and had fantasized the lifting of the burden of power from his shoulders by circumstances. Andrei, his father's old valet, had come in with the breakfast tray and had looked at him a fraction longer than usual before bowing. Ruzsky had rushed to telephone Rodzianko in Petrograd to offer the Emperor's services as honorary minister in the Duma and prime minister with full executive powers in home affairs: there was no alternative, even Alice had telegraphed from Tsarskoe Selo: MAKE CONCESSIONS. He sat at his desk waiting for the answer from the capital, fingering the paper knife he had bought many years before in Paris: one morning he had wanted to look at the city free from royal protocol and had been taken to the Faubourg St. Honoré, where he had caught sight of the paper knife in a jeweler's window. The precious seventeenth-century dagger had passed from hand to hand down the centuries to finish in the possession of a tsar on an October morning in 1896, in Paris, and it was still on the desk in the Imperial train where it had been for the last twenty years. Like the steeple of Pskov Cathedral over there, beyond the carriage window at Dno, the small station whose name in Russian meant "abyss": a fifteenth-century steeple that had survived different regimes, wars, invasions to stand in front of the train where the Tsar sat waiting by the telephone to know his fate.

He fingered the gold and ivory paper knife: during the wait, everything was still possible. He wrote his name in the notebook and blotted it, then upturned the blotter to check his name, seen backward. Yes, they were still one and the same thing, his power was still there, in those characters set down on paper, in that signature reproduced on the proclamations which for almost twenty-three years had been posted up at street corners in every language of the empire. The engine was quiet, the furnaces had stopped burning during the two-hour stop. The writing desk, a gift from the Shah of Persia, had been well-polished, the silver gleamed. The clock, secured to the gray padded walls, had stopped at 11:36; the relentless ticking irritated him and one of the first moves on that journey had been to stop it. Why on earth did they wind it, they should know by now that the sound was irksome to him. He slid a finger over the clothespress, not a speck of dust. He rang the bell on his desk; the newspapers, let them bring him the papers.

An appetizing smell reached him from the kitchen two carriages along, where Kharitonov and the other cooks, as if they were still living two months before, were preparing lunch for all the retinue . . . that's right, there was lunch to come, to get through . . . by then they would know the answer, the decision would have been taken once and for all.

Later, on the telephone, Rodzianko had spoken clearly of the possibility of saving the monarchy, but only with the Tsar's abdication in favor of his young son Aleksei, with Nicholas's brother Mikhail acting as regent. While Ruzsky spoke, Nicholas's face gradually smoothed out and lit up, all tension seemed to leave him. There was nothing left to do but gather, in the shortest possible time, the opinion of the generals on every front: the decision whether to abdicate or not depended only on their answers now. Alexeiev and Ruzsky left the train once more to make contact with every corner of the empire and the Emperor prepared to wait again, alone in the Imperial suite. When Ruzsky brought the telegrams from the generals the morning of Thursday, the second of March, after breakfast, and a valet laid the silver tray with them on the desk, Nicholas calmly made use of the ivory and gold paper knife, careful to slit the flimsy blue paper of the Imperial post where it would not tear through the stamp that detailed the hour, the provenance, the number of words, all information that was already more important to history than to him. The Tsar was no longer there, insofar as his position depended on the generals: those flimsy bits of paper were horribly unanimous; he had to abdicate. He got up from his desk, went to one of the windows and lifted the curtains: he was stifling, but lifting the curtain, opening the window, was not enough. Perhaps he should leave this station. And if he should feel equally suffocated in the open countryside, where could he go? He would have to abdicate on a train. So many important Russian events had taken place on trains after all.

He remembered the night after the arrest. They had come to the train at the headquarters in Mogilev where he had gone to take leave of the army; it was the eighth of March. That night he had retired to the Imperial suite and had begun to undress slowly in the glimmer of the icon candles next to the prie-dieu. Alone, a prisoner, not knowing where he was going and whether they would be stopped by some rebel unit in control of the tracks, he would never get to sleep. He sat on the edge of the bed. They were passing through some major junction, he could feel from the jolts as they crossed the switches, from the more frequent bends: the subtle pleasure of trying to guess the way with eyes closed, deducing from the movement and speed what could be the route. The crystal glasses and jug of water for the night tinkled. That water, that remained there, sealed, unused, during the day, enchanted him. It seemed a reproach, an invitation not to let go, not to submit to the events but to consider them from a new angle. Everywhere in the world, throughout the centuries, there had been men like him, prisoners who did not know either the reason for their condemnation nor the time of execution. If only the door would open and the Tsar of Tsars would walk in, and he could finally meet the great friend, the great father who explains and enlightens, stronger, taller, braver. . . .

Now the train slowed down, wound like a snake into a station and seemed about to stop, but gathered speed once more, fled as if escaping from attack, slipped away from a station occupied by disbanded troops. The lights on the Imperial train were all extinguished now. In front and at the back revolutionary soldiers already represented the new power.

On March 9 he prepared himself to leave the train for the last time. It had come to rest, like a barely perceptible wave, on the usual reserved siding, at Tsarskoe Selo. He did not take the French dagger, while the valet Andrei and Prince Dolgoruky gathered together papers and closed bags and cases: he left the paper knife on the desk that it might reach the hands that wielded the new power and open for them the telegrams that power reserves for its representatives. He wanted to leave the objects to influence whoever came after him, as they had influenced him. He imagined he saw the train of power puffing still through the vast expanse of Russia, although without the gilded arms and the blue lacquer. In this way the long imprisonment with his family began, the long calvary that brought them to these July days in the Ipatiev house. He had become more taciturn, rarely taking part in his children's talk. Aleksei had noticed it particularly, and frequently wondered how they would be celebrating his birthday on July 30, when he would be fourteen, on the very same day as his cousin Ernest of Bavaria. The year before there had been a little party, and even the escort of soldiers had taken part, singing and dancing. But now? What would they do for it? The soldiers who were guarding them now were nothing like those of Tobolsk and Tsarskoe Selo: these were hostile to him and his family in a thousand small ways; they had even called his father "Nicholasky the Bloodthirsty." How different soldiers can be. At Petrograd the cossacks of the Imperial guard had been so glad to see his father when he went down to the mess next to the Winter Palace. They did indeed love the Tsar and himself, the Tsarevich. But could there be soldiers who did not love the Tsar? What tsar could they love, then?

The head of the guard here in Ipatiev's house was Jurovsky, an ugly lanky fellow from whom no good could be expected. But one day this man, so ugly and surly, had stopped by the doctor to discuss Aleksei's health, even showing an interest in the treatment he was undergoing for hemophilia. His mother had interpreted this unusual behavior as a sign that things were going to improve. But his mother didn't really understand the situation. At table, where they ate with the guards, her silence and haughtiness froze everyone; she was so disdainful, sitting upright and pale-faced. Mother was not kind, not like his father who sometimes smiled, sometimes exchanged pleasantries with the Red soldiers. His father sometimes seemed no longer to be able to endure discussions with her, those discussions that took place at night, in their room where Aleksei pretended to be asleep. She swung from a state of febrile excitement to terrible depressions, times when she thought her husband was hiding something from her, as if there were some consolation to be found in an alternative reality known to the Tsar and deliberately kept from her. How many times in those months the self-contained, disdainful mask had slipped as soon as the daughters left after their ritual good night. The insistent, hysterical whispering plagued Nicholas; it was an added, constant torture.

—... because there must be a way to reach the Whites, make contact with them, you know it perfectly well, Nicholas, you know it, you know whom you can trust in this house, in this town, who can keep a secret, who is only waiting for a signal from our windows to come to our rescue. You've seen, Nicholas, you've seen how careful they are not to let us open the windows, how they keep them always shut ... we can't stay here, idly sit by, we must do something, we can't let ourselves be murdered like this, Nicholas, think of the children ... tell me you know we shall be rescued, don't keep it hidden from me, because you know, you know, how it will be done, you've always known and you've never wanted to tell me, never wanted me to know. ...—

Before she was overcome by a fit of weeping, Nicholas would rise and go to call Dr. Botkin; an injection plunged Alice into a restless sleep not unlike the strange certainties of her waking state. Nicholas mutely waited for the silence, and on certain nights would begin daydreaming once more, his thoughts and questions: who were the revolutionaries really? Lenin's name was one of the many that was brought up again and again like a piece of driftwood, beached with one wave, to be swallowed up in the next one's retreat. Who knows where Kerensky was now, carried away by that vast seaquake that had dragged everyone into chaos.

Once, years before, when his father was Tsar, in the days before the decision had been taken to thwart attempts on the Tsar's life by having him travel in a train preceded and followed by identical trains, the Imperial convoy had been forced to a halt because of a bomb discovered at the last minute. The guards had caught the terrorists fleeing across the fields near the tracks. Contrary to the norm, Alexander III had wanted to see the prisoners, and they had been brought to him, their clothes torn in the recent scuffle with the guards. To the fifteen-year-old Nicholas, the prisoners had appeared quite beautiful. In a state of mind between admiration and terror, he felt absurdly attracted toward them. He would have opened the door if he could have made off with them, escaping the crowd of police, aides-de-camp and railwaymen, and spoken with them, not only to find out why they had done it, but to get to know them, walking together through those woods to which they had tried to flee. He had run one of the last carriages so as not to see them being dragged off. One especially he had never forgotten, the smallest of the four, blond, thickset, with slitlike green eyes: Alexander Ulianov. He had often dreamt of him, and always in the same situation: on the beach at Livadia on the Black Sea. He would see him coming out of the water, smile at him with his half-closed eyes, come close and engage him in a long wrestling match until he had thrown him and he was black with sand. Then he would disengage from Nicholas, leap to his feet laughing, dive into the water and disappear swimming. The dream always ended there. He was a revolutionary, but Nicholas could only say of him that he was a wrestler, a better wrestler than himself, with green cat's eyes. After they had resumed the journey, his father had called him and asked him why he had left so abruptly before he had finished questioning the terrorists. He had not been able to answer, and the Tsar had interpreted the silence as a sign of weakness and childishness, great faults in a tsarevich.

No one in Russia could understand the condition of a son of the Tsar. Two men in Russia stared at each other as in a mirror: the Tsar and the son of the Tsar. The first could do anything, the second nothing, not even in the most intimate and private areas of his life; those too were subject to constant instruction and control. Any muzhik was free once he finished work, to go in peace and enjoy a little glass of something, blaspheming to his heart's content against any mishap of the day; but the Tsarevich could not have even an hour to himself as long as the Tsar was alive. Then, one day, the day the father died, the son, the most enslaved man in the empire, became the most powerful man, the only free man in the empire. It was a miracle that had been repeated for century after century and had preserved Russia from the specter of freedom. A new but identical power was born of the existing power; in a deliberate exercise of repression, freedom was extinguished as soon as it was born, and Russia had existed for centuries without yielding to dangerous illusions. Because it was also an illusion that the Tsar was the one free man, although the Tsarevich only realized this when the moment came, as he waited for the court to bow and call him Imperial Majesty. The first orders, for years imagined to contradict the parental ones, reverted within days to being exactly like the father's, and on that day the Tsar's freedom came to an end, on the day he could no longer look forward to his days as Tsar.

Now, however, both Tsar and Tsarevich had lost their freedom, prisoners in Ipatiev's house. Nicholas could not know that his son considered him responsible and would not forgive him for what had happened.

The sailor Nagorny had not been around for a while now, to curb Aleksei's exuberance and follow him wherever he wanted to go and guard against the consequences of a fall or an accident. The duty to carry Aleksei had passed to Nicho-

las. The Tsar could not imagine that his son did not understand the abdication, just as Nicholas's father would not have
understood it. Aleksei loved soldiers; when he was with them
he never felt ill. Far from considering himself not up to the
position of emperor because of his hemophilia, the boy had an
absolute conviction that he was destined for that role, in which
he saw his father performing without the authority and the
confidence he would have brought to it. He would not have
let Granduncle Nicholas go to the front to win glory in combat, he would have gone himself and led his soldiers against
the Germans. And his father had abdicated for him too, in
favor of Uncle Mikhail who was so unenthusiastic. Had his
father any right to do it? Only because he was a little weak
and had lately found it difficult to stand? And yet his father
knew how much he liked to go to headquarters and listen to
the generals outline their problems to the Tsar in front of a
vast map of the empire, moving little flags representing regiments this way and that. One day during an inspection in the
Dnieper region in the first summer of the war, Aleksei and his
father had left the automobiles of the escort and gone toward
the river. They had found a little beach of dark sand and
Nicholas had undressed, inviting his son to do the same. They
had played in the water together, never moving from the
shore. For a while, swimming, splashing, vying with each other
as to who could keep his head below water the longest, they
forgot the chauffeur, the generals, the aides and the military
advisers.

—Father, what if the Germans were to turn up here! Can
you imagine their faces if you told them that you were the
Tsar and I the Tsarevich—and we without a stitch on!—

—They would laugh and go away.—

Aleksei stopped laughing, suddenly serious, and asked his father:

—But they would take us prisoner if they saw us in uniform, wouldn't they? Aren't we the same naked?—

—It's the war.—

—Well, then, if we were all naked, does that mean there would be no wars?—

—I thought you liked playing at war?—

—Oh, yes, I do, I do.—

And Aleksei had hurried up the riverbank to get dressed, having remembered his father's promise that he could join him today as he reviewed a regiment that was leaving for the Eastern Front, the Preobrazhenskii Regiment, the one commanded by the famous Colonel Prince Ypsilanti.

3

As soon as the Preobrazhenskii Regiment began its march toward Tobolsk on the last Sunday in February, Prince Ypsilanti appeared among his soldiers mounted on his horse, and during those first few days, it was as if an angel went ahead of them, changing the weather to a mildness unusual for Siberia. Why has the snow stopped falling? How long can this quiet spell last? Ypsilanti kept worrying as he looked up from his tent each night at the star-filled sky, the night as limpid as it practically never is at that season: the days pass, the horizon recedes into space, and Russia is still Russia.

Smoking by the fire with his officers in the evenings the colonel encouraged them to tell him more about their units than they would put down in the stiff daily reports handed to him through his chief of staff. It seemed as if he almost took pleasure in making them feel uncomfortable, as if he enjoyed challenging the good humor that had spread among the troops moving through the vast white expanse, still and peaceful, with no wind and no storm.

—You must ration the alcohol more strictly. The weather

will certainly not last and the soldiers must be ready for the worst.—

—Prince, forgive me, but really one can't give them less. . . .—

—I'm telling you, they'll need it more in the future. I noticed in precisely your unit, Khabalov, things that I don't like. Your soldiers are behaving like drunks from first thing in the morning. What can make them so cheerful? They sing, they challenge each other, they look for a thousand pretexts to see if they can get ahead of the other units. There's no hurry in a march like ours, there's no first, no last, they'll understand it soon enough. . . .—

What a strange man . . . isn't it better for everyone that the troops are in good spirits and not asking too many questions? Khabalov sat thinking in silence, and as if reading his mind, Ypsilanti came out with a murmured phrase, staring fixedly ahead:

—I don't think it's a good idea to ignore totally one's fate, to move toward one's future without understanding it, not even for a twenty-year-old soldier. . . .—

The days passed in the tranquillity of a magic spell. The long columns of the Preobrazhenskii left on the white, barely recognizable roads for Tobolsk and the Urals footprints and wheel tracks that seemed to disappear immediately, as if a spell had been cast, as if no one had passed by there, as if that impossible march wanted to leave no trace and someone wanted to draw the regiment most faithful to the Tsar, the glorious army of Peter the Great, even farther away from civilization. Every morning, having drunk the coffee prepared by his orderly, Alyosha, son of an Armenian father and a

Parisian mother, who spoke only French with him, the prince calculated the distance, spreading out the map of the empire to mark the miles they had traveled. The march was more and more like sailing the open seas, he thought; and as he opened the folder containing his most important documents, his eyes almost invariably fell on the roll of the Supreme Command, on which the names and ranks of his dearest friends were printed in gold, senior officers like himself, scattered everywhere at the head of their regiments in that war so remote from his own regiment, which formed a useless outpost to nothing. With a twinge of nostalgia he would run his eye over the familiar names that for so long he had not mentioned: Dolgoruky, Alexeiev, Danilov, Kolchak, Nepenin ... He wondered where they were fighting at that moment. Perhaps by the side of the Emperor, if His Imperial Majesty really was in danger. Or perhaps at their posts, on the Galician front, near the commander in chief, Generalissimo Nicholas Nicolaievich? He had heard nothing of them for more than a year now. He felt as if a high wall had been erected, silently, day by day, month by month, between him and the world. His soldiers seemed to him at times weightless, bodiless, mere shades. Those were the moments when their fate and his moved him and he would catch himself looking up at that pale blot in the sky behind the clouds, the weak Siberian sun. But as soon as reveille sounded, five minutes after he was up, he would come to himself again, and whatever his sense of tragic futility in those precise gestures, in those hoarse commands, however much aware of the empty ritual in the rhetoric that in a few minutes brought perfect order to the finest Russian regiment, he would enjoy his moment of pride and hope, he would forget Vachitino and think of the arrival at Tobolsk. It was another day to live, another day of searching for the Tsar. Still another, incredible day.

The soldiers even found the time for combat drill during the longer pauses. Each company had had to be reorganized because of the deaths on the march to Vachitino, but now, during those exercises, it seemed as if the regiment had found an efficiency that made Ypsilanti proud. All that was missing was the enemy. The bravest, the most resolute, battalion was the Third, which had endured the fewest losses, thanks also to Captain Karel who held them together with iron discipline. In that battalion were those most determined to reach the Emperor wherever he might be, the ones who were least likely to give credence to rumors of rebellion against him. Ypsilanti found himself most frequently venturing forth among them in his nightly inspections. He felt as if there he found once more the faithful heart of the regiment that had everywhere demonstrated its superiority to the enemy.

He was all the more surprised therefore when one night, hidden and unrecognizable in his cloak, he stopped behind the kitchen tents and overheard two soldiers.

—Do you think we'll make it?—

—If this lasts we'll surely make it to Tobolsk; I can't wait to sleep in a real bed in a warm house, above the stove, far from all these conceited officers, where there are women and a lot to drink. . . . I've had my bellyful of this war, I can't stand it anymore.—

—But what war? If we get to Tobolsk, then there'll be the fighting, it'll be anything but women and stoves, the Tsar is waiting for us there to reenter St. Petersburg. . . .—

—Really, I can't understand you, really, I don't at all. Yes,

yes, of course we'll follow our Tsar, but can't you stand the idea of stopping a month in a town? You know we didn't even manage to find a bed in Vachitino, a decent house, a brothel, nothing. Tobolsk is a big town, Feodor has been there; the Tsar will just have to wait a little; how will he make his return if we haven't had a rest? Anyway, can't you see he's the one who needs us?——

——Vanya, what on earth are you saying? Are you mad? It's us looking for the Tsar! He doesn't need you, or me, or any of us . . . or anyone. . . .——

And Vanya hadn't replied, had sat silent, and the two had rubbed their hands over the fire. From where Ypsilanti was hiding he could see their bearded faces in the light of the flames. He felt as if he were seeing them for the first time: one of them must have been wounded on the chin; there was a long white furrow in the beard just under the lips, as if the hair refused to grow over a scar. He must be the one who had been frightened by Vanya's boldness, the shyer and more loyal one. The other, as lean as an eel, was better groomed, cleaner, with a trace of good looks on his tired face.

Ypsilanti walked slowly away from the kitchen quarters and lifted his eyes to the sky that showed stars through patches of cloud. Tatars, Mongols, Uzbeks, Circassians, Persians, how many people had crisscrossed that land without leaving any tracks, just like the wake from a ship that closes behind immediately. Perhaps conversations like this between two sentries had taken place before, on another night long, long before, so long ago that it was as if no one had spoken at all in that vast desert, beneath those identical stars. He who was in command of all those men, those who believed in Christ as well as those who believed in Allah or followed Jehovah, he was like time that erases everything, he could forget he had heard them, he could leave them, there, in front of the fire, forever. There was no tsar waiting for them at Tobolsk, he knew that well enough. But this too would be forgotten, the heroic and dreadful lie.

He thought of the last time he had seen the Emperor at Tsarskoe Selo. Yes, he had seen him, he had not dreamt that; he had stood in front of him talking for half an hour the day after the declaration of war against Germany. He had not dreamt it. The Emperor had told him of the last phone calls to the Kaiser the night before. He had not dreamt it. Ypsilanti felt he had to tell himself this again and again, as if someone nearby, near one of the fires, were whispering that no, it was not true, that that face with the blue eyes and the beard threaded with gray, that half-forgotten face was not the face of the Autocrat Nicholas II, the Tsar of all the Russias.

The months passed and Ypsilanti's thousand men had a sharper sense each day of having crossed another frontier, as they had before Vachitino. But at what point? In which part of the empire? And into what new territory?

One evening Ypsilanti gathered his officers in his tent for the daily reports. They had left Vachitino many weeks before, but the general feeling among the officers was that the five hundred versts they had marched since the isolated town to which Ypsilanti had thought the devil had led them, had taken them no nearer to Tobolsk. Yet the soldiers had marched well, there could be no complaints of laziness or inertia. Exceptional discipline and exceptional weather had allowed them to come this far. But where were they? The officers, just like the soldiers, would have been hard put to say where they were, because the map of the empire was blank about the endless region adjacent to the estuary of the Ob. There was not one name of a town, no sign of a chain of mountains, not a lake, still less the dotted red line of the railway. There were only, in large Cyrillic script, the first two letters of the Russian word SIBIR, the S and the I. There they were, above the mysterious sibilant of the word written on the map compiled at the Military Geographical Institute in St. Petersburg, an exact copy of one dating back to the days of Catherine the Great.

—Supposing we really were to succeed in reaching Tobolsk, sir?—

The strange question came from one of the officers while the colonel was platting on the map the position noted by his chief of staff, and checking it with his compasses. Ypsilanti knew that voice, it was Karel's, and without raising his head from his plat, he hissed through his teeth:

—I don't know what you mean, Captain. It's obvious we will reach Tobolsk. The Emperor waits for us. I don't want any more questions like that.—

The silence that followed seemed to underline the folly of the answer. So, had he decided to pretend with them too, accomplices as they were in the necessary lie? Or had he really gone mad? He no longer wanted the truth. Khabalov turned to look at the commanders of the Second and the Fourth battalions, and gestured to Karel to keep quiet and leave it to him:

—Forgive an old soldier, Prince, but those condemned to death are not denied their last wish. . . . Are you the magician who has brought spring to the Siberian winter? Satisfy our curiosity about that, and then we'll be able to believe anything you tell us. . . .—

—You're being insolent, Colonel. I won't allow you to

speak in this way to your commander. Out of respect for you I will pretend not to have heard that remark. If we had been at Supreme Command, however, you would not have got away with it.—

But we're not at Supreme Command, the old colonel thought, staring down at the camp table of the Paris-educated prince, looking at the framed portrait of the Emperor, the glass with Ypsilanti's silvered coat of arms, the ivory-handled whip, the pens, the compasses, the sextant, all those signs of a civilization so removed from that tract of land where not even the furrows made by the wheels of the wagons and the footprints of boots remained on the road half-buried in snow, to be an indication that there still was a capital, a Supreme Command, an Imperial army. Of course, Ypsilanti could pretend he had not heard his officers' questions. There was no greater authority than his here. He could act like God in that desert, he could even believe he could crush the truth and impose a fiction. And anyway, in their situation just what was the truth? The soldiers seemed to be convinced—indeed hypnotized, as if fear of reality had been transmitted even to them, secretly, and they were beginning to believe the lie in preference to the truth. He had overheard some of them even today, quarreling among themselves about who would mount guard outside the Tsar's palace when they arrived in Tobolsk. One of them had stopped in midsentence, just as the memory came back to him of the one time he had seen the Tsar inspecting his unit at the front:

—. . . and meanwhile there is nothing, nothing to be seen down there, nothing at all, never anything . . .— and he had turned with an oath, swearing, toward the horizon veiled by low clouds lit by the sunlight that was so unusual at that time of the year. And one by one the soldiers had stopped talking and had turned, leaning on their rifles, and stared at the distant flat line of the horizon.

Then one day, the frozen earth split, spewing out its secret humors, and water and mud at first paralyzed the column of marching men. Spring burst as violently and suddenly as a fever. They had to build bridges, ramps, hurdles and duck-boards—long hours of work for the military engineers, the sappers and bridge builders; they had to bridle the insane land that in a few days had transformed a static world of ice into snaring quicksands. Only such operations saved the artillery and the wagons from a sea of mud, as dangerous as the bite of the frost. And now summer, the short, harsh Siberian summer, gave to those young bodies a sluggish desire for rest, a thirst for pleasure and for sleep that was more devastating than the weariness of winter.

Ypsilanti was happy. He observed the enthusiasm of his troops; he thought the march had been a success despite some victims, that the strange unnatural weather that had worked in their favor had finally disappeared, giving way to a season that seemed more natural. It didn't matter that Tobolsk was still far, that during this last stretch they still had not come to a telegraph station, that they had got lost again. He was happy anyway.

—Alyosha, bring me my cigars and help yourself.—

The orderly, who had attended him for ten years and more and had gone with him on journeys abroad, brought him the round box with the engraved initials, but he did not sit, he stood, smoking: Ypsilanti knew he should not invite him to sit if he wanted the man to be at his ease.

—What do you say, perhaps tomorrow we can go and

shoot a few birds, eh?—— He knew Alyosha's passion for hunting. In France he had been his beater on fox hunts, and the prince liked to tease him when he was in a good mood.

—Oh, no, Your Excellency, we mustn't now, it's the nesting season, it's not good to shoot while they're mating.——

—You're right, Alyosha, you're right. We must leave nature alone, not disturb her, we've flouted enough of her laws, we've enjoyed enough of her miracles. . . .——

Alyosha did not answer, but took a long drag at his cigar— he was used to the prince's strangeness.

4

Nicholas stood looking out from one of the windows in Ipatiev's house onto the driveway, the side away from the shooting, in case something might happen, a miracle might occur. But his family had already benefited from more miracles than any human could reasonably hope for. When the hemophilia had manifested itself in the newly born Aleksei fourteen years before, it had been a miracle to save him, a miracle that had later been repeated through the agency of the same man, Rasputin.

How Alice had loved Rasputin! Nicholas, on the other hand, although convinced of the protection the man gave his son, had not lost sight of the danger Rasputin was to the monarchy. The starets had stolen charisma from Nicholas in exactly the same way Simon Magus had wanted to steal it from Peter. The powers he had no longer been able to use had not lain unused, had looked for someone else through whom they could be exercised. Such powers had belonged to Aleksei the Calm, Nicholas's favorite among his predecessors, the father of Peter the Great, and had indeed been invested in all real kings. If today the monarchy was in decline it was because kings had become functionaries, presidents, men who no longer knew how to use these powers. He would have wanted that power intact, he did not want to accept the supreme gift of second sight, the unique human science, in a rough and uncouth peasant like Rasputin. Would that he still might be able to refuse certain reforms of the Duma for the one simple reason, as he replied to the president of the chamber, that "the heart of the Tsar is in the hands of the Lord and cannot go wrong." This had been the will of centuries and this was still the wish of the Russian people. But Alice had thwarted him in every possible way. To have given birth to an heir considered an idiot by all the chancelleries of Europe had almost driven her mad, and she had lost sight of their dignity, sacrificing it to Rasputin to obtain the health of the Tsarevich. Perhaps that had been the original mistake, not to have fought against the infiltration into court, so close to the seat of power, of a magic not sanctified by the providential function of the monarchy.

One autumn evening shortly before the outbreak of war at Tsarskoe Selo, the Imperial family had wanted to dine alone with Rasputin. The young grand duchesses, dressed in the black silk of mourning for the recent death of their father's uncle, the Grand Duke Aleksei Alexandrovich, seemed even more pale and fascinating to the wild Siberian monk; at times his bright feverish eyes could not but betray a hint of pain and anxiety, as if not even the especially kind attentions of the Empress, who had wanted to serve him personally, succeeded in putting him at his ease. The Grand Duchess Tatiana, the second of the Emperor's beautiful daughters, aroused in him secret thoughts and desires; he thought he saw in her something different from the enervating beauty of her sisters, some ancient, strong and mocking quality visible at moments in her capacity to sustain and almost to challenge the famous magnetic gaze of the starets. Alice was distracted, her attention strayed constantly back to the nearby bedroom where her son lay in the most recent crisis of his illness.

Nicholas had wanted to discuss the Russian Church with Rasputin: he was aware that the monk tended to despise the mass of priests as superstitious parasites, idlers incapable of miracles. Rasputin wanted to force a confession from the Tsar, that miracles are the only guarantee of the authenticity of the Church, and that the Church only existed where there were men able to perform them.

—But don't you think, my dear Grigori, that if our Church were to support itself only on miracles it would mean that men no longer believe in God?— Nicholas asked that time.

—Why on earth should it, Little Father?—

—Because it would mean that people no longer had real faith, simple belief in portents and miracles. Where does the freedom to believe or not to believe go to then? Don't you think that the greatest possible portent is faith itself, that strength to live and hope which imparts its richness to everyone, each man and woman, not only to certain exceptional individuals?—

Nicholas would have liked to add, in face of the evasive answers by Rasputin, who had immediately understood where the Emperor was trying to lead him, that just as the divine risks nonrecognition, so the Russian people had to continue to believe in their corrupt and parasitical Church which relied on their faith for its own purity. The Tsar was thinking of his own power as well as that of the Church, both of them threatened by the violence of Rasputin's miracles, while the monk seemed uncertain, anxious to change the subject, and moved his eyes restlessly around the table, having stared straight ahead throughout the discussion. The Tsaritsa came to his rescue and the conversation turned to Aleksei and prayers for his recovery. And while the Little Mother, in a voice hoarse with anxiety and pain, begged him to pray, Rasputin was aware once more of the contrast with Tatiana's haughty and mischievous eyes.

Rasputin's distrustful and resentful mien had sunk deep into Nicholas's memory. At the moment of leave-taking, having knelt in front of the Tsar and having been helped quickly back on his feet by Nicholas, Rasputin fixed him with his terrible magnetic eyes:

—Little Father,— he said, —all is over if there are no miracles.—

And the threatening shadow of mockery was a gloss on this prophetic allusion to calamities. The mistake had been to have given, out of pity for son and mother, a share of the power to the man who with miracles killed the monarchy, the Church and the faith. Rasputin was not the only Siberian monk to have been murdered, two years before, by Prince Felix Yussoupov and Grand Duke Dimitri; that was the beginning of an evil destined to spread far and wide, beyond the empire. The spirit of such a mentality pervaded the air in a tendency to expect the most out of reality, to perceive it with all the five senses, with every pore of the skin, instantly, with no half-measure or compromise. Nicholas was sure that people contaminated by such a way of seeing, so impatient of reality, incapable of asking but used to claiming, would destroy a whole world. He was not sure he would like to live in the new world they would fashion; perhaps he would not even have succeeded in imagining how he could have fitted in, were it not for the vital, restless presence of his children, in their fiery young adolescence, that compelled him to reproach himself for such acquiescence.

There was so much time to think in that prison, so much emptiness to fill, identical days spent on the first floor, in the five rooms with the dirty windows, walking in the sinister garden almost wholly in the shade, with its withered and niggardly plants, its gnarled branches. There was a pomegranate tree in the garden against the wall—whose fruit was beginning laboriously to ripen and looked poisoned. Behind the last hedge where the other houses of the street were, the perpetually barred, shuttered windows seemed intent on not divulging who it was they had seen held prisoner in Ipatiev's house.

Who was left in the town? Was there anyone alive? Where did the inhabitants hide? Did they know the Romanovs were there? Did the rumor leave them completely indifferent? Did they too want miracles, these subjects of the Tsar? Did everyone want a miracle from the Tsar who did not even know how many more days his jailers were giving him? This was what Russia wanted, the devil had been sent to him too, to the Autocrat of all the Russias, to tempt him, to see if he could resist and not invoke a miracle, twelve legions of angels to rescue him, the Tsaritsa, the Tsarevich, the Grand Duchesses Olga, Tatiana, Maria and Anastasia, and all the Imperial family, scattered and tormented throughout the lands of Holy Russia! What kind of testimony could be wanted from the Tsar, prisoner? Was this a test on which the future of his people depended? How could he believe that? Should he tempt Almighty God, yield to seduction, ask, insist, shout, learn from Rasputin? Alice had frequently said so in those worst moments of Aleksei's illness, as she embroidered the starets's shirts.

—Nicholas, you should learn from our friend, you should be as decisive, don't hesitate when giving an order, be terrible, you are the Tsar—remember! Look at Grigori, look how he towers, how he petrifies whoever dares look at him. That's how a tsar should be. . . .—

5

That evening Vassily played one of the most passionate tunes he knew on his harmonica for his companions. It was the song that was sung in his village in Crimea for the feast of Saint Spyridion, when the flames from the burning of the stubble blazed along the riverbank all the way to the Feodosiya gorge up in the mountains. His father had taught it to him as a child, before he fell ill and disappeared into one of the hospitals in the city where they took those who like him had taken to drink. His father had been the village musician: there was no pot or pan, no fife, no reed that, touched by those magic fingers or blown into by those thick lips, was not transformed into a devilish instrument that compelled anyone who heard it to start dancing:

—Remember, music belongs to the devil, that's why it's so powerful, that's why it's so irresistible . . .— he had told Vassily once, reeling down the steps from the tower where he had been to ring the bells of the church with his ears plugged so as not to be deafened and a bottle of vodka so as not to lose inspiration. Twice a year, at Christmas and on Saint Spyridion's Day, his father and his uncle Hilarion would get drunk up in the bell tower, outringing each other for all the village to hear, with their madcap irresistible rhythms, weaving a harmonic counterpoint into the strokes of the clapper until many peasants from the neighboring villages would be attracted by the lure. Just like the inhabitants of the village, the companions of the forty-seventh tent began to dance and clap in rhythm, incapable of keeping their legs still at the sounds of Vassily playing. They forgot Ypsilanti, the taiga, friends lost on the way, the march, the war.

—I swear, as soon as I get to Tobolsk I'll drink so much vodka that I'll sleep for three days. Enough of the poison Ypsilanti doles out,— Misha shouted, pausing to take a long draft from the bottle, —and I'll leave all my alcohol with you for safekeeping, Ignatic, 'cause you don't like the stuff!—

Ignatic, the young Georgian gunner in the First Battalion, sat in a corner near Misha's cot and stared out of big blue eyes at his companions who laughed loudly, passed the bottle and clapped their hands, nodding toward Vassily to go faster.

—Aren't we going to wake everyone at this hour?— Ignatic asked Misha, almost more with his eyes than his voice. Misha burst out laughing once more.

—Listen, listen to the little lamb. Don't you know that everyone is making merry with us this evening? Be quiet, everyone, and listen a moment, for God's sake, if you can still manage it. . . .—

They were all drunk already, but after a lot of grumbling they all shut their mouths and either stood or sat on beds or lay on the floor to listen. Yes, it was true, the merrymaking was general, but not only on the part of the men, not only in the tents where men's voices seemed to embody a sort of undertone interrupted by bursts of laughter immediately cut short. Out of the night to overwhelm them came a crack of snapped branches, a sound of running water, the shudder of hidden forces, the echo of strange calls and bellows, as if beasts never before encountered by man had gathered there, in the forest bordering the great plain where Prince Ypsilanti on horseback had raised a white-gloved hand to call a halt for his regiment.

The forest had been sighted at sunset, after a blistering day. Ypsilanti had seen it through binoculars—a few specks of green barely visible on the uncertain horizon. Gradually as the trees took shape a new frenzy had spread through the troops. There was the taiga: true, they could lose themselves and die in there, but they could also live, hunt, gather wood, enjoy the shade of a tree, listen to birds singing. Rapidly the word spread that the Tsar was there, beyond the forest where, only a few more days' march away, lay Tobolsk, the city of Saint Aleksei. Everyone felt as if the march were coming to an end. Some lived in villages just beyond the forest, in the district administered from Tobolsk: Berezovo, Sosva, Ivdel. The names flew from mouth to mouth. Yes, in many tents that evening there was carousing, just as there was in Vassily's tent. Vassily's friends were convinced of it and began to drink again. Vassily resumed his playing.

—Come on, Ignatic, come on little one, let's dance a little.— And Misha, while the others clapped in time to the music from the harmonica, bent toward his friend who shrank back, not wanting to get up from his corner.

—See how lovely he is, the little lamb Ignatic? Don't look at him too much though, because he blushes immediately . . .

you know, the other night he was tossing and talking in his sleep . . .—

—No, no, Misha, please, be quiet, leave me alone . . .—the Georgian begged.

—Oh, come on, what's wrong with dreaming of your mother? Yes, the little angel, he was dreaming of his sainted mother and begging her in his sleep not to think he'd forgotten her even though he hadn't been home for three years. He told her he was going to be home soon and would take her to Moscow to see the Red Square and the towers of the Kremlin and to pray in the Cathedral of the Annunciation. . . .—

—He better dream himself up to date, your little angel, if what the Jews said is true. Who knows what kind of hell there is in Moscow now?—

It had been Efim who spoke, the sergeant major blind in one eye, who fired from his left shoulder. The others looked at him without answering. No one wanted problems that evening, they had had enough: cut off from the world, with so many companions dead from the cold, with less and less food, they did not want any one-eyed man spoiling the party. He'd always been different, never happy, always arguing, not very pleasant. Probably that was why he was still a sergeant major at nearly fifty, after all those campaigns of which he was so proud, showing off his wounds and the bandage over his eye.

But even if they did not answer, for a moment all the men thought the same thing: that blasted war that had taken them so far, so far they could no longer feel as if they were soldiers in a war. It was not only the Tsar they were looking for after months of marching, after that damned village of Vachitino. Perhaps they were looking for proof that they were still alive, that was why they had to drink this evening to forget. Summer, at least summer had come, and was real, a real hot Russian month of July in the year of Our Lord 1918. . . .

—Enough, Misha, I don't want to, why don't you leave me alone, what have I done to you?—

Ignatic's beautiful innocent face seemed even more innocent when tears of fury ran down his cheeks and Misha held him tight, forcing him to take dance steps.

—Beautiful Ignatic, you're as beautiful as a woman. But we won't tell this to the women when we get to town, we won't tell them, don't worry. You'll see how many will come looking for you at night, as soon as they see you come into town. . . .—

Misha became even more excited at the laughter of his ever tipsier companions. He was fond of Ignatic; he reminded Misha of his brother Nikita who had died at twenty of petechial typhus in the first year of the war, on the Masurian Lakes. He had heard the news from his mother in a letter that reached him over six months ago, when they were still on the Eastern Front, before the regiment had vanished into Siberia. It came on the tenderest of mornings, while he was convalescing from a shrapnel wound to his hand, sitting back with his legs dangling from the bed, with the tent flap open to welcome the gentle sunlight. When the corporal tossed him the letter he had not noticed Ignatic looking at him with envy, for no one ever wrote to him from home. Heedless of Ignatic, Misha opened the letter slowly, to savor every second of his imaginary return home, and had immediately recognized his mother's handwriting, the neat hand of the schoolteacher in the village in the Yaroslav district. When he had read of the death he felt a confused terror, as if something had broken and he was not sure he could get up and move as he had done before.

He must have changed color because Ignatic rushed up to him and clasped his good hand. That was why he was fond of him and continued to torment him.

—If you don't stop, Misha, you'll be sorry.— Misha released him and Ignatic slipped free and ran outside.

—What do you think, will we cross the taiga or circle it?— Kiril took advantage of a quieter moment, while Vassily paused for breath and had a drink, to throw out the question.

—I can't imagine the old man wanting to circle it. He'll want to cut through it, zac, like that, as if it were bread and we were the knife.—

—Oh, but he can't be that stupid, he must want to save his skin.—

—Why, you think he does? Ypsilanti? You know that my battalion commander lets me in when he's holding his staff briefings, to make the coffee because no one can make it as strong as I can. . . .—

—Yes, and so? What have you heard?—

—They're dissatisfied. I heard them talking as if they consider him a madman who wants to die; the colonel never mentions his name in front of me, but it's as clear as daylight. Even the officers call him "the old man," just like us. . . .—

While Kiril told this story, Efim drew near and listened as if aroused from some deep reflection. His eyes brightened: it was as if the talk awoke something familiar in him and he had been waiting just for that moment to talk to them at last. But Vassily started to play again with renewed vigor and an energy that stopped all talk and Efim, annoyed, went out to breathe some fresh air. He was so angered by those drunkards, incapable of understanding the situation they were in. That night of general euphoria seemed a bad omen to him, as if the spirit of the regiment that had been his life for so many years, as if the spirit itself sensed dangerous consequences in the complete abandon of this one evening. These troops have been out of the firing line too long—what kind of soldiers have we become? Where is the war? I've not fired a shot for more than a year and continue to polish away at my rifle every day. It's all Ypsilanti's fault, he's the one who's taking us away from the Tsar with the excuse of looking for him, he wants us away from what is happening in St. Petersburg, he knows what's going on, of course he knows. And these poor fools get drunk just as he wants them to.

Efim had been smoldering with resentment against the prince ever since he had learned that his promotion to warrant officer for which his captain had recommended him had been blocked by the prince himself when they were still at the front.

—He can get his promotion when he's retired. I don't care for sergeants who are as old as the colonels in my regiment.—

Efim knew this had been the prince's comment and since then his frustrated ambition had transformed him into a damned soul.

There was another man in the regiment who like Efim, brooded resentfully against the prince. It was Colonel Guderian of the First Battalion. Efim was convinced that Guderian too could not stand Prince Ypsilanti; he had seen him too many times emerge from private discussions with the prince. And he was well placed to observe not only because his single eye could only just hold its own against the excessive tension of a mind constantly alert to discover who else, like him, was being shabbily treated, but also because of his duties as staff sergeant in the commander's office. Guderian wanted to see the prince dead, just as Efim did. He had been reprimanded for negligence, distraught behavior, carelessness, lack of authority, too many times. Ypsilanti's voice was loud when he lost control, especially with superior officers, whose offenses he could never condone as he could the ordinary soldier's.

Efim had let slip a confidential remark one day after one of those stormy interviews. He pretended to pick up a piece of paper in order to draw near to the colonel who was standing there, in a fury, stiff as a ramrod, wiping the sweat from his forehead.

—It's sheer and utter madness, sir,— Efim murmured. But the officer pulled himself together and with one icy look, screwing his monocle back in place, made the half-blind non-commissioned officer feel the full distance between them. And Efim, without understanding why, had sprung to attention in front of this officer of His Imperial Majesty.

6

———

At that moment, in Ipatiev's house, the sound of a whistle was striking the Emperor's ear. A train was crossing the Urals going toward Moscow from Eastern Siberia. Men were traveling on that train, free men. Perhaps free. Yet he too, on the way to Ekaterinburg, had been free to ask permission, of a filthy Uzbek guard who had answered with a grunt, to open a window. Was it real life, the one that had already passed by, 1897, 1909, 1912, all the years, months, days, that had vanished? Or was it all there, gathered in the pronouncing of the words needed to ask whether a window might be opened? Life gave itself in the one last greedy draining of the cup, and that was itself always a loss, a hemorrhage. His life no longer existed, as used up as the boots Trup kept on polishing, trying not to wear them out. But life became worn, showed its warp and woof. He, Nicholas thinks, is as much a has-been as those who, without knowing they are no longer alive, go by on that train, pass through the town of Catherine where the Tsar is prisoner with his five children. It seemed as if indeed Ekaterinburg was the gateway to Siberia through those black mountains, the place of mythical hate and rebellion, full of resentful people. There, at the Urals, Europe, Russia, the world ended, and immediately another world began. He, like his predecessors, had ruled over Europe and Asia, on this side and on the other side of the Urals. And now the Romanovs existed on the border, at the limits of the empire, though still within it. —The world never ends, . . .— Aleksei murmured, looking up one night at the stars that his father was pointing out to him through a window of the prison. His father nodded and continued giving him the names of stars, then looked down at the small Tsar who would never be Tsar in a world darkened by the new moon, in a night that would have the duration of a dynasty. What a strange destiny to be waiting for the outcome in the farthest corner of Europe, "at the edge of the world" as Alice always said, for she had no love for the Asian regions of her empire.

And yet to any exile to Siberia, to be assigned to residence at Ekaterinburg had been a special favor to obtain from the Emperor; to be called back from Siberia to this mining town carried with it the hope of seeing wife, children, mother. Aleksei had asked his father how many versts there were to St. Petersburg, how many days' journey, and then he went and looked up the map of Russia in the geography book. He would gaze, stare, at the green for the plains, the pale yellow for the hills, the pale blue for the seas, the darker blue of the rivers, all the colors down to the dark, dark brown, the almost black of the Urals. He would run his finger along the fine red line of the railway and make the journey to St. Petersburg; he would hear the sound of the sleeping cars, tu-ton tu-ton, tu-ton tu-ton, tu-ton tu-ton, see the bridges, the stations, hear the whistles, the switches, the brakes applied, and see there, in the distance, down below, the glorious gold spire of the Peter and Paul Cathedral.

—Mother, we're home,— he had woken crying one night. The boy had a favorite toy, the wooden model of a steamboat, memento of an extraordinary encounter. With it he would travel past the bed and the chairs on the Black Sea, always leaving from Livadia. Aleksei had never traveled to Europe, had never left Russia: his parents had never felt like taking him with them on tiring state visits. But once, on the Black Sea, he remembered two Turkish warships escorting the Imperial yacht *Standart* until they had come to yet another ship where the Tsar had met the Sultan. Nagorny the sailor had said:

—We're no longer in Russia, we're in Turkish waters.— And so the experience of the world for Aleksei had been of an intensely blue, intensely flat sea, two cruisers, one slender ship and an old bent man wrapped in white and gold cloth, with a hooked nose and a quick voice like Natasha, the parrot Aunt Elizabeth had brought from America. It was the Sultan of Turkey, who had returned the visit of the Tsar, climbing aboard the *Standart* toward evening to share a meal. A strange man, the Sultan, surrounded by a swarm of young boys who invaded the ship in a flash, and by very few ministers. Seated at the table, he let his beard be stroked now by one, now by another, of the youngsters, who snatched away from him, laughing, the best pieces and who poured him champagne.

He had given Aleksei a marvelous warship, a steamboat almost a meter long, with wooden sailors in the shrouds and crow's nests, a double row of guns in gold set broadside and a great white crescent on the ensign. He had given him the gift at the beginning of the meal—Nagorny had immediately been ordered to fetch him—and a dark bony hand as slender as a claw had stroked his chin. Inexplicably, of all Aleksei's toys, the Sultan's steamboat had been the one to accompany him all the way to Ekaterinburg.

During the day Nicholas tried to distract his son by talking of the end of the war that would also be the end of their imprisonment, and spoke of the regiment to which he had always thought of sending him, the legendary Preobrazhenskii. In talk, everything fell into place with time and with the help of the Whites.

—Can you hear them, Aleksei?— he would murmur. —Can you hear how they are shooting down there? They are our faithful subjects, there are many like them, all over Russia.—

Aleksei looked at his father without comment. The Preobrazhenskii, who knew if they still existed . . . better for his father to think that he believed him, he was so pale, his beard so full of white hairs; the dark-ringed eyes seemed so much larger, those beautiful eyes of his father. Nicholas understood the expression in his son's face and fell silent, turning to a book; and Alice's voice would reach them, as sharp as a knife, and even though he could not make out the words, the tone alone told him how dissatisfied she was with him; and Olga would take the brunt, the gentle, affectionate eldest daughter, always ready to smooth out differences and relax tensions, especially her mother's. The heavy, large features of Grandfather Alexander III were softer and more serene in Olga's face. She had already forgone marriage once to be with her family, had turned down the proposal by the Crown Prince of Romania, Carol. Nicholas could not stop himself from imagining how different his daughters' lives might have been if he had agreed to the many proposals. Carol of Romania had not given up after Olga's rejection, and had turned his attention to Maria.

—Absolutely not,— the Tsar had said laughing. —Maria is still only a schoolgirl, she's only sixteen, Your Highness, you must understand, please. . . .— Then came the turn of Edward, the handsome Prince of Wales, son of his cousin King George, but nothing happened. Olga hadn't wanted to hear of it that time either:

—Father promised not to force me and I don't want to leave Russia. I am Russian and mean to remain Russian.—

And you have remained Russian, my poor daughter, and you will always remain Russian. You could have saved yourself and perhaps your family too. Perhaps, who knows, Lloyd George would have listened to a future Queen of England, would have sent a ship from his glorious fleet to St. Petersburg to rescue my children. In his fantasies he never sought his own safety on that ship. He felt that the war was still in progress and that even the revolutionary government needed his presence in Russia: at times he would not believe that the peace treaty of Brest Litovsk had really been concluded; he did not accept the possibility that a real Russian, however revolutionary, could sit at a table with the Germans and hand over half the mother country with a signature to a treaty. It must be a lie by his jailers to draw him into a trap. Alice thought so too:

—Don't trust them,— she would tell him at night. —It's some ploy by the revolutionary government to put pressure on you.—

He knew the Bolsheviks came from distant countries, like Switzerland, Italy, France, after years and years of exile: they were no longer Russians, they no longer had any knowledge of their country. Only in this way could they have concluded such a treaty. Russia was the only country in Europe to have escaped the Enlightenment and that was her strength. This was a belief that grew in him as he traveled around the empire among the millions of people, but it was also a conviction he derived from the dead each time he went into the Peter and Paul Cathedral on the first of November, the anniversary of his father's death. The dead continued to offer themselves up, he drew strength from them. The sarcophagi of almost all the tsars and tsaritsas of his dynasty were there, lined up, the men in uniform, the women in capes, beneath the white stone of the lid, surmounted by the gold cross and the eagles, all waiting for the trumpet of Judgment. But there was a continuum from them to God that was demonstrated by Russia in all its myriad forms: Russia did not belong to Europe, or to Asia, but to God. He felt dizzy when he stepped into that church; twenty steps in that chapel was like crossing over two hundred years. He had wanted to show the place to his cousin the Kaiser, sometime, to demonstrate to him how silent true greatness is. Wilhelm had always been the most insufferable braggart of the crowned heads of Europe, and Nicholas had never been able to stand his arrogance. He could not forget the last time he had heard that voice on the telephone at Tsarskoe Selo, one night at the end of July 1914, while the armies of all Europe were preparing to clash. Nicholas had just gone to bed, in the Alexander Palace, after a day of dramatic tension. At around two he had been woken by old Andrei, his father's valet, who had told him the Kaiser was on the line from Berlin. Wilhelm had already sent him two telegrams that day, a day so full of consultations with English and

French allies and of angry exchanges with the Austrian and German chancelleries. While the Kaiser gradually raised his voice, Nicholas had for some seconds forgotten the high-pitched tones of his cousin, suddenly absorbed in the crack-lings of the line, the background noises. He could see the thousands of versts that separated Berlin from St. Petersburg, regularly spaced by poles topped by the Imperial eagle, right to the frontier. And within these vast spaces, some hundred million people waited for war or peace: men like him, women like Alice, boys like Aleksei, old women like Maria Feodorovna, the Empress Mother. Not a single one of them was unknown to him; he could not at that moment avoid the issue—he knew each one of them as long as he held power of life and death over them. During a sudden pause in Wilhelm's outpourings, he regained full concentration and recollected his cousin's last words; he replied that it was impossible for him to act otherwise, faced with the mobilization of the Austro-Hungarians. And he was ashamed for the Kaiser who, by exploiting the ties of friendship and of blood, tried to gain a few hours for his field marshals; he knew from the secret service that Germany's declaration of war on Russia was already signed. When finally, after inconclusive and deceitful promises of further consultations at the earliest opportunity, it became clear to Nicholas that war had begun for 120 million subjects that night, he became convinced that his father had been right in his belief that a king could not use a telephone without compromising his regality, because that infernal instrument abetted the duplicity of the worst class of actors like Cousin Wilhelm, who could pretend and deceive in a tragedy like war.

7

Let me go, let me go or I'll shoot. Ypsilanti is a fiend, he's a devil, he's the one who made summer in winter ... let me go, let me go, damn you, let me go or I'll kill you. You're his serfs, you've sold your soul to that devil, that fiend, I know you're all against me. Let me go or I'll cut you all to pieces.—

They were trying to grab the crazy soldier before he could shoot: soldiers rushed in from all sides, new arrivals were signaled to stop and keep quiet, those nearest were warned to clear out; there were frantic exchanges between Captain Karel and five of his men who were trying to draw the madman as far as possible from the camp perimeter. The captain had realized immediately, even before Prince Ypsilanti arrived on horseback, how dangerous it was to the soldiers' morale that those wild shriekings should go on. The madman was a hussar, assigned to the horses of the Headquarters and Services Squadron. Mild, peaceable, the first to volunteer for the most onerous tasks, the last to complain about the discomforts of the march. Nothing much was known about him: he came from a village in Karelskaya Maselga, where night is as long as day for six months of the year. He had certainly seemed a little strange lately, but then who had not in the last few months? At night he would suddenly wake and start rummaging through his sack as if he were afraid of no longer finding something he could not do without, and he would look around with surly eyes if he could not find it immediately, fixing his comrades with an accusing gaze, blaming them for the loss of that precious object, that fragment of mirror. And when he found it, and they had thrown a boot at him to stop him being so fidgety and let them sleep, he would light a stump of candle and stare at his reflection for minutes at a time, stock-still.

Only then would he calm down, having made sure his face was still sitting on the neck, framed by the hair, punctuated by the eyes so very much like his mother's. His mother had died when he was still a boy, and a large photograph still remained at home, in which she smiled, she smiled as he now smiled while he looked at himself, then made to put out the candle and lie down. He remembered the day they had gone to the village from their house on the cliffs, to have that photograph taken of his mother who had been unwell for a while. Though he could not have been more than four, he had never forgotten the long brightly colored dress and the black shawl, the glass door into Bilibis's shop. Bilibis came from a land far away in the south, sold a little of everything, even women's clothes and shawls, and had a camera in a recess behind the counter. When his mother had gone in, he had waited outside the shop; Bilibis had given him a bar of chocolate and told him to wait outside for his beautiful mommy. He had seen her through the shop window, laughing as she loosened her shawl, before going behind the counter, where Bilibis had his camera. But Bilibis's hand on her shoulder had seemed blacker even than the shawl, so dirty and ugly that he had dropped the chocolate and without making a noise, on tiptoe, opening the door just enough, he had slipped in. At first the material of that lovely brightly colored dress had rustled and hidden the murmur of words uttered so softly and so quickly he was not even certain they were spoken words. He gazed at the candy jars on the shelves, the cupboards made of spruce wood, the casket of flour, the rolls of fabric on the counter, the rows of harpoons, the fishing nets, the portrait on the wall—it must have been of Bilibis as a boy, in the heart of a big forest in his native land: already he had hard lackluster eyes, dark as his hands.

It had been a cry, a sound weaker than a cry and louder than a sigh that had made him tremble from desire to lift the green curtain of the recess and look at his mother who was having her photograph taken. And in his anxiety he had knocked against a harpoon that had been resting against the counter, sending it crashing to the floor with a pile of tins. He had run out, and a little later she had emerged, red in the face, hot, without the shawl. Bilibis was still smiling at her through the window when the boy gave his mother his hand and walked away, without him having seen anything behind the green curtain. The photograph had been hung at home by his father some months after his mother died that same year. And there she was, smiling not at him but at Bilibis with hands as black as his eyes; not at him who resembled her so much, who was trying to reach her, to lift the green curtain of so many years before, while he looked at himself in his fragment of mirror.

But apart from the nighttime strangeness, his mates had noticed nothing particular about Piotr Ivanovich Ostov.

—When did the wretch start all this?— Ypsilanti thundered while a platoon of riflemen surrounded the madman who seemed to be heading toward the taiga, beyond the outermost tents.

—An hour ago I heard a great noise from one of the infirmaries, your Excellency, the one for the Third Battalion. But it was too late to stop him, he had already grabbed a weapon and ammunition. He went to the infirmary yesterday because he wasn't well.—

And still the unbearable yells persisted:

—Ypsilanti is the devil, let me go, let me go home, I don't want to die.—

The shouts had drawn a large crowd of soldiers who stood silently by, watching. Ypsilanti, conscious of his rank, considering it inopportune to be there listening to those insults, spurred his horse and turned back. A decision had to be taken immediately; the soldiers could not be left under the spell of those cries that split the air and let in specters which the prince knew all too well hovered already over the camp in front of the taiga, specters in search of minds ready to embody them and give them a voice. He called the man's commanding officer:

—Who knows him well?—

—Perhaps one of his tent mates?—

—Well, call him, quick. If we don't find a way to quiet him, I'll have to have him put down.—

The man's three tent-mates arrived at once, but Ypsilanti could find nothing the terrified men said that could be of use, and he was about to dismiss them and give the order to shoot before the poor madman fled, when he noticed that the eldest of the three, as he saluted, showed a bleeding finger.

—What have you done to yourself?— he asked, almost inadvertently.

—I cut myself with Piotr's mirror. . . .— And then he muttered, but still loud enough for the prince to overhear: —And now he'll not wake us again at night to look at himself in the mirror, poor devil. . . .—

Ypsilanti made the soldier tell him in detail of that strange habit, staring into space as the hussar talked. When the man finished, the prince turned abruptly to Alyosha and told him to bring the large mirror from his tent, the one that stood next to the portrait of the Tsar and Tsaritsa, under which new recruits had always sworn their oath of loyalty. A few minutes later the oval-gimballed mirror was placed upright on its wooden stand, as near as possible to the crazed soldier. Ypsilanti hid from the madman behind a gun carriage, in such a position that he could give orders to Karel with a wave of his white-gloved hand.

The madman noticed the big mirror set up between himself and the regiment, and seeing that the soldiers had drawn back and were no longer chasing him, seemed to become curious. He gently lowered his rifle without letting go of it, took a few steps and was in front of his reflection, tilted slightly toward the ground, with a full backdrop of the first trees of the taiga: he had never seen such a big mirror; up to that moment he had merely known his face in a fragment barely the size of the palm of his hand. Now he seemed frightened and fascinated by the discovery of his body, as of that of a stranger. He moved his legs, his arms, touched himself, as if to enter into that image too vast to be taken in by the eyes alone. He seemed to want the help of his hands, as if his eyes were not enough, and suddenly, with a strange smile, he began to undress, placing his weapon within easy reach. He had finally realized to whom his mother was smiling in the photograph: Bilibis was there in front of him, in the mirror, against the taiga, just as he had been in that painting that had hung in the shop twenty years before, the picture on the wall between the harpoons and bales of cloth, between nets and candy jars. Bilibis was he.

The clothes fell to the ground slowly, first the jacket, then the beret, the belt, the shoes, the trousers, until he was naked. He smiled with half-closed eyes, bending to pick up the shirt, rubbing it against his skin, whispering incomprehensible words, the same words that had been murmured behind Bilibis's green curtain. That curtain had been lifted now, he had gone through, he was with her, now, forever. He would take her with him into the taiga. He turned slowly, abandoning mirror and rifle, and moved with measured light steps.

To Ypsilanti he no longer seemed one of his soldiers, one of the men who had followed him and obeyed him through so much; he was an animal free to run under the sun, a creature of another world. Captain Karel, next to his platoon of riflemen, made the sign to take aim and turned to Ypsilanti, waiting for the order. But the prince, with an incalculably slow gesture, lowered his gloved hand in a signal not to shoot, and remained watching the man until he had disappeared into the taiga.

That night the clearest moonlight for many months lit the Preobrazhenskii Regiment lost in Siberia. But the news of hussar Piotr Ivanovich Ostov's sudden madness excited many sol-

diers, traveled from mouth to mouth despite severe warnings
by the commanding officer of the riflemen who had witnessed
the scene. By midnight there was no one who did not know
the words, the gestures, the orders, the sequence of events.
Everyone knew that a crazed soldier, a hussar, had dared say
that Ypsilanti was a fiend and that all of them were his creatures, his slaves. The mirror next to the portrait under which
so many of them had sworn fealty to the Emperor
in front of Ypsilanti, as he stood still and impenetrable in
ceremonial uniform and otter-fur cloak, yes, that mirror had
served the poor madman to undress and gaze at his body
naked as the day he was delivered from his mother's belly, had
served as he undressed and contemplated himself in it before
he disappeared, muttering nonsensical words. Could it be that
the prince, the terrible colonel who had coldly threatened so
many in the regiment with death throughout this terrible war,
who had acquired a reputation for being an unflinching leader
in so many campaigns, could it be that he should have spared
this poor soldier's life? After all, he may have been mad, but
first and foremost he was a deserter, he had abandoned the
army for the taiga under the very noses of his commanding
officers, and after having insulted them. Yes, he was certainly
free now, their companion, he was down there among the tall
trees of the taiga, from where the powerful scent of pollen and
flowers reached the camp, from where the calls of large beasts
and smaller animals could be heard. But he could only be free
to lose himself and die in there, like everyone who had ever
entered the taiga unaccompanied. And yet all were tense, listening; would they be able to distinguish, among the disquiet-
ing sounds, Piotr Ivanovich Ostov's voice calling to his
companions, to his comrades to come to his rescue, to help

him return to the camp? Because surely he would not call them to catch up with him, to follow him out there, where he was. . . .

Those who suffered most from his metamorphosis were the hussars in tent 72 of the Headquarters and Services Squadron, his mates. Feodor, having had his cut attended to, the one that had enabled Ypsilanti to save Piotr's life, sat looking at the deserter's empty bed, the icon and the fragment of mirror in a corner under the oil lamp, the mirror that Piotr would no longer hide in the sack after contemplating his reflection. At that moment the other two arrived.

—Do you think he'll be back?— one of them asked.

—Why should he? Even if he could still understand something, why should he come back here?— Feodor lashed out in fury.

The others shook their heads, shrugged their shoulders in silence. But they knew he was not wrong.

8

He could not read. He could not endure it anymore: the Whites had been shelling since two o'clock this afternoon, and Nicholas thought they seemed much closer than yesterday. He tried to control himself, to show the same indifference when Jurovsky came into the room, his black eyes staring at the floor.

—You'll have understood that it's the Whites shelling; they've been at it for days, but the Reds are putting up a good resistance. And in any case, whatever happens, you, Nicholas Romanov, you are with us and you'll go with us wherever we go. I've come to tell you not to get excited at all that shooting, in case funny ideas come into your head. Your daughters never stop asking to open the windows with the excuse of the heat. By God, you better tell them to stop, tell them this house has no windows. . . .—

Jurovsky hit the desk with his fist, leaning forward toward the Tsar who did not move, who continued to look at those poor filthy windows.

—There are no windows and there cannot be any, do you understand? And if we opened them, who knows, Nicholas

Romanov, whether you wouldn't wish they were still shut. There are cellars too, you know, in this house. Remember that.—

He really seemed wrought up, the ugly thug. Something was worrying the man, who was normally so disciplined, something that stopped him from making use of his usual weapons of intimidation, those insistent, repeated stares, the silence. The Reds were obviously not as much in control as they made out; the cook was right in anticipating changes, in trying to bribe the permanently hungry guards with choice morsels to gain more information. But if the Reds were not masters of the situation, they were still able to lord it over them, and still more furiously. They must not delude themselves, Jurovsky was right.

Now the jailer went, whispering something to the guard that made him laugh, turning around to look at the Tsar. Miserable cur . . . He would have to explain to the girls not to show any interest, whatever might be going on, that it would simply worsen their situation. If only they had some news about what was happening there in the direction of the shots, if only they could know whether those Whites were regiments of his army or rebels against the new government . . . it was enough to drive them crazy, this uncertainty, this swinging between hope and fear. Nicholas tried to remember which of the most faithful regiments could still be stationed in the regions closest by. He borrowed the geography book from Aleksei; he too looked up the map of the empire.

There, in the region of the Southern Urals and in the Kirgiz Steppe, his father's plan of deployment provided for the stationing of 200,000 to 250,000 men against a possible Turkish attack. Suddenly, reading the name Bogdanovich, the capital of the district, he remembered that at the time of mobilization back in '14, a cavalry unit, the Volinsky, had been stationed there. Alice was its honorary colonel. Bogdanovich was three hundred kilometers from Ekaterinburg. In the Kirgiz Steppe, on the other hand, were stationed Uncle Paul's cossacks. And so, on the thread of what he remembered of his regiments, he reconstructed his monarchy on the map, just as Aleksei traveled the Black Sea on the wooden ship given him by the Sultan of Turkey. Nicholas passed in review the Semonovskii, Ismailovskii, Litovskii, the Oranienbaum machine-gun Regiment, the oldest and the bravest regiments, till he came to the most legendary one of all, the one founded by Peter the Great himself, the Preobrazhenskii Regiment. He could see it, on a faraway morning in June 1890, in full battle gear, lined up behind its officers in its four battalions, with its standards and standard-bearers, its band and its commanding officer paying his respects and presenting arms. He had spent a whole month with that regiment on his return from a journey to Asia with his brother George. At the time, they were holding joint summer maneuvers with the French; he was still Tsarevich—it was the days of Mathilde, the dancer in the Imperial ballet. That summer he had succeeded in getting Mathilde to join him at Vilna where the Preobrazhenskii was stationed.

Every evening after dinner at the officers' mess, Nicholas got into his carriage and joined Mathilde in the apartment they shared with his cousin, Grand Duke Alexander, and with Larisa, Mathilde's violinist girlfriend. There was great accord among the four since Nicholas had begun to share in his cousin's military life. Mathilde was small, lively, full-bosomed, with an arched neck, brown curls and vivacious, intensely blue eyes; she had dramatic and unpredictable variations in mood. It seemed to Nicholas that when Mathilde was gripped by some ancient sadness, it would possess even her clothes, her bed, her jewelry; it would alter her countenance, her voice, the color of her eyes. It was, Nicholas thought, as if she had the power to turn wine into water, to alter the cooing of doves in the garden to desperate keening, and then, suddenly, a few minutes later, full of gaiety, she would turn the water back into wine, and the sobbing of the doves into the tenderest mating coos.

Throughout their nights of love in Vilna, Nicholas had tried to understand from where the woman drew the incredible power that had affected even his father, that evening of Tchaikovsky's ballet in St. Petersburg. He it was, after the performance, who had summoned her to the Imperial box to meet the grand duchesses and the Tsaritsa.

—Where's Kschessinska?— the Tsar had asked. And she had come up to the Imperial box, with her heart in her mouth, amid the envy of her dejected companions, and under the complacent eyes of the dancing teacher, who relived her own presentation to the Tsar, the previous Emperor—because there is always a presentation to the Tsar for those who dance as if they could dance forever and never fear to grow old.

—You are the jewel of our ballet,— the Tsar told her, raising her from her perfect curtsy and taking one of her small hands to a chest covered with decorations. Nicholas was coming into the box just at that moment.

—Nicholas, take the young lady back to her dressing room. It has been a great joy for us to attend your performance; we are grateful, mademoiselle.—

It had all started in front of the Tsar, who was usually so

indifferent to the arts. If Mathilde came into a room, immediately all were aware of her presence and turned their heads. Her beauty was only a partial explanation of her effect; there was an enchantment about her that was irresistible. Once, entering Warsaw together on a short journey, Nicholas had said in their carriage, holding her tight:

—My darling, how wonderful if all the town knew of our entrance and the people were to come out of all the houses to greet us, and so crowd the squares that we could barely make our way. . . .—

—I would prefer the town to come to a complete standstill, I would prefer to be able to stop it by an act of willpower. And then you would see the air still, the clouds stationary, the birds unwavering in the sky. The River Vistula itself would cease to flow and beyond the gates even the sheep no longer move and the shepherd lifts his hand to beat them with his crook and remains paralyzed. . . .— And she made the gesture of shepherd with his stick, fixing her gaze. She could just see it all, she said. Nicholas was amazed, stared at her, held her even tighter, as if afraid she might vanish in the morning air.

Mathilde was interested in everything, constantly searching for new amusements and oddities with which to entertain Nicholas when he was free of duties. At Vilna she had wanted to meet an ancient fortune-teller, famous for having predicted from the tarot, for the Empress Eugénie, the victory of Sevastopol and the defeat of Sedan during the first years of her husband's reign.

—But, my darling, do you really believe this nonsense?— Nicholas asked shyly.

—Of course. It's easy enough not to believe it. . . . I'm sure it'll be very interesting, and we mustn't joke about it, it's very serious. . . .— Another sudden mood-change, observed Nicholas; she's about to burst into tears. When they met again that evening, Mathilde begged him to stay with her, not to go out with Alexander and Larisa, she had to talk to him.

—What is it, my dear?— Nicholas asked soon after, closing the door of their room.

—There's an army in your future, an army that will look and look for you to help you, Nicholas; it will wait for you for months, maybe for years, faithfully, ready to die for you, waiting for your orders, but the orders will not come. It's invincible, but it's without you, and will not believe those who say that there is no longer a tsar in Russia.—

—What do you mean, Mathilde?—

—What I said, my love. I saw it with my own eyes at the fortune-teller's today, before she even spoke a word to me. . . . It's terrible, no one can set it free from its loyalty to you and you know nothing. And no one can warn you that it waits for you.—

—You're mad, what nonsense is this?—

—I'm not crazy, I wish I were. I see what will happen to you . . . and I won't be there. . . .— And Mathilde fainted, leaving Nicholas stunned and anguished. When she came to a little later, Nicholas asked her to explain better, but the dancer, in one of her sudden changes of mood, ran to open a bottle of St. Raphael, inviting the Grand Duke Alexander and Larisa, who had just come back, to join them. She never returned to the subject until the last months of their affair, when the European press was already anticipating the engagement of the Tsar's son to Alice of Hesse. One night she whispered to him:

—Remember that the soldiers will reach you, they'll

become smaller and smaller and no one will recognize them. . . .—

Mathilde had vanished from his life like a vision as soon as the engagement with Alice had become official and Alice had converted to Russian Orthodoxy and taken the name of Alexandra Feodorovna; his mistress's strange words seemed to have vanished with her until the day Nicholas II discovered them again in his memory, searching on the map where the regiment might be that was ready to die on an order from him. Now he understood that for those with access to the divine, time is always present, everything has already happened, everything is as still as the Warsaw and Vistula the dreaming dancer had seen in her imagination. He was beginning to think he knew more than his father, that he had seen places his father had never visited. Could the regiment be at Cistopol? Could the regiment in search of the Tsar be there? Or in Samara? Could it be the army of cossacks stationed on the Aral? From name to name, from town to town, loyalty to the Tsar emerged again from the map wherever Nicholas paused to look. He felt as if, like Mathilde, he was somehow penetrating things; the name of the town, divided into three syllables, SA-MA-RA, somehow gave its key to him; he had been Emperor of the other one, which had been the seat of a bishop, a tribunal, a college of the nobility. Now, on the map, he took possession of a magic city of sounds, without history, somehow much more his own than the other one, so bound to the centuries and to stone.

Perhaps I'm going mad, he thought, called back to reality by the entrance of Alice; perhaps this is the way one goes mad, looking at the atlas of a sick child. But she'll take care never to forget our situation, there she is now. Alice was trying to find out what Jurovsky had said; she had just been told he had come to see her husband.

—Are they going to take us away again? Did he have orders for you from the government? Did he see Aleksei? Did you talk to him too, Doctor? Don't hide anything from me, I beg you, Nicholas.—

Poor Alice, whatever could I possibly hide from you now? But he had to answer so as to reassure her, quiet the agitation that affected him so deeply.

—My dear, he came up to tell me to keep the windows shut. The Whites are drawing near . . . but don't worry now, let's go down into the garden.— Alice looked at Nicholas without listening to him; his behavior was strange, unusual, he seemed much more energetic, there was something in the eyes . . . there was a strange tremor in the hands, he was paler even than usual. He seemed taller, more severe, as if a new strength, a strength he had never shown, had been released. Oh, but he did not fight like her, she was not going to let herself be beaten. She had never accepted, resigned herself, to what had happened, not like him, who was so easy, so agreeable to their jailers. Her husband had already accepted everything before it happened.

Going down into the garden the Imperial family found the guards ready to follow them along the paths. Nicholas gave his arm to Alice, behind them came the grand duchesses, the doctor, Trup, and Demidova, the Tsaritsa's maid. The hourlong walk took place in thoughtful silence barely interrupted by the chatter of the girls, up and down, up and down, first up the path where there was the damned pomegranate tree that had difficulty bearing fruit, then back along the hedge of sycamore, down to the benches. Three soldiers, without belts and with their shirts unbuttoned, smoked as they stared down from the open windows on the second floor. Alice, as rigid as a statue, sat on the bench and called her daughters.

—Your Majesty, it's best to walk, best for the health,— Dr. Botkin insisted. And the Imperial group started their walk again between their guards. After a while Nicholas went back upstairs alone to collect Aleksei. His son had not been able to walk well now for months, since a fall on the stairway at Tobolsk, which had given him a turn for the worse.

—Why are we going down, Father? They're bad, those soldiers, let's stay up here,— Aleksei said as soon as Nicholas came in.

—It's not good for you to be cooped up inside all day. Don't you want to go out?—

—Out where, Father?— And the boy looked at the back of his father's head as Nicholas carried him piggyback, looked at the beautiful head like the one on the stamps stuck on the postcards he used to send to his cousins in Hesse to show them pictures of St. Petersburg and of his father at the same time; like the crowned head on the rubles. He had never been quite sure what they were used for, those rubles. No one in the household seemed to carry them around.

Now, in Ipatiev's house they continued to do without rubles in exactly the same way as in the Winter Palace. One day in Finland he had gone fishing on the Louisa estate with his father and his father's cousin, Kaiser Wilhelm. He was not used to being still for hours in the fresh air and could not wait a minute longer for the fish to be caught.

—Are you on the rubles too, like Father?— The question had made the Kaiser smile.

—Certainly. Only, they're not called rubles in Germany.—
—What are they called, then?—
—Marks.—
—Will you show me one?—
—I'm sorry, I don't carry them; my aide-de-camp will have some.—

And the prince of Hohenlohe had handed a wallet over to the Kaiser. The child, astonished by his cousin's answer, before seeing the marks had spoken gravely:

—Then you too are poor. We're all poor, then.—
—Yes, Aleksei, and one day you too will be poor, when your portrait is on the paper money of the state. Come on now, be quiet and let Wilhelm fish.— Nicholas had settled the matter. Aleksei had tried to picture his own crowned head on the rubles, but he immediately felt sad, because it meant that his father would no longer be there. There could not be two tsars. Aleksei did not know he had in fact joined that long, seemingly endless line going back in time, of those men who came one by one. He too had been Tsar of all the Russias from three to nine one day, on March 2, 1917. On the blue Imperial train, at Pskov, Nicholas had abdicated in favor of his son who had become Tsar Aleksei II for six hours. But, tormented by the thought of his son's health, when the delegates of the governing committee arrived from Petrograd that evening at nine to act as witnesses, he had revised the act of abdication, this time in favor of his brother. Alice had approved the fact that Aleksei had never been told, horrified that he could even have been considered as a real heir.

—You could have saved him this comedy; let's hope he never gets to know of it.—

—If I had not done it, don't you think he could have reproached me with it one day?—

—When, at the next hemorrhage? Only Rasputin could
have secured him the throne if he were still alive.—

Rasputin. Alice must really have loved the man who
vouched for her son's life; sometimes Nicholas was convinced
of it, thinking there were two Alices, one who had loved him
before the birth of Aleksei and the other who had shut him
out, incapable as he was of healing her son, and had given
herself to the man who could. The second Alice was only
mother, the first had also been wife. Nicholas had loved
the first one and shielded the second, especially through the
revolution, on account of her inability to understand. She
couldn't understand how peasants could rebel to the point that
she, the Tsaritsa, had to walk up and down a little path in a
prison garden. When she had got off the train at Ekaterinburg, the peasants at the station had frightened her. They had
had to force their way to the waiting cars through muzhiks
that pressed in on them, pressed in, in silence. She had had to
make her way through their cloaks and mantles, their greasy
boots, through their stench. These were the peasants who
every year came to Tsarskoe Selo from the four quarters of
the empire, hat in hand, bearing gifts in their baskets, to sing
around the great crib at Christmas, to sing under the direction
of the priests. Now they said (she had read it in the newspapers at the outbreak of the revolution) that all the land
would be given to the peasants, as the most absurd nineteenth-
century writers had proposed. This is a hope that will kill a
few million of them. Then the power will be strengthened, and
since Nicholas does not know how to wield it, it will go in

search of another tsar. But from what world could a peasants' tsar come? Alice was convinced that it was a member of the Imperial family, hiding behind another name. Louis and Antoinette had been betrayed by Philippe Egalité: what snake had the Imperial family harbored and nourished? Paul? Mikhail? Alexander? or Nicholas, the commander in chief? Which of the cousins, of the uncles, was hiding among those extraordinary commissars of the people, whose train had seemed like a devil rushing to snatch its quota of souls as it hooted them out of its way when it exercised precedence and rushed past theirs which was taking them to prison in Tobolsk? They had shed the gorgeous uniforms of the empire and donned the jackets of the Red Army, but they continued to pursue their lust for power—never mind if it meant shedding the blood of the Tsar and his family.

—Oh, the sooner they get rid of us the better,— Alice had reached the point of whispering to Nicholas, to whom she talked in this way at night, in their room on the second floor of Ipatiev's house. It was always a long list of recriminations that Nicholas endured in silence.

—You shouldn't have given command of the cossacks to Paul, you should have understood his ambition, his desire to emulate your grandfather . . . he's always felt he was the heir ever since our alliance with France. And then, all those years spent in Paris and Switzerland, do you really think he stayed in Paris for the women? Can you believe that? He met Bolsheviks in France, he began to conspire against you there. . . .— Those ravings of Alice's did on certain nights succeed in evoking the spirits of his relatives, and Nicholas saw them all prisoners in those very cities they had loved and in which they had been made welcome. No, no one had betrayed him. Their way of life had stopped them from entering a world that had opened up, just as it prevented his children, even if they were to make themselves smaller and smaller as Mathilde had said. Where could they escape from it? An angel could save them, only an angel could rescue them from this year 1918, to take them back a hundred, two hundred years. . . . But if Russia remained solid in space, she kept moving in time, and the Tsar had been successful over the centuries only in securing her outward form—her mountains, her plains, her lands as vast as his power. They had looked at each other, the Tsar and the land, looked and stared at each other as enchanted as two absorbed lovers.

It was God's power that had stopped time, not Nicholas. Halfway between his subjects and God, Nicholas had not seen on Russia's face what the gentlest of blue eyes required without the mediation of time. The empire was only half eternal, a failed suicide. These were Tsar Nicholas's thoughts one evening in Ipatiev's house, when he found himself lifting his head slowly: There is an angel singing, even the guards smile, but it's Anastasia, my little Anastasia . . . , and the icy walls melted, someone was nuzzling the hearts of the house's residents like a dog leaping for joy at the return of his master. But who was returning? Why had the maid stopped sewing and the grand duchesses paused in their reading? And then the doctor and Aleksei rushed into the room . . . and what silence down on the ground floor, in the guardroom. Anastasia sang, and it seemed as if her whole life were gathered in that song, her time as adolescent, mother, queen, grandmother, all caught fire in that song. It moved death and made it withdraw, just as the sun called into birth by the rooster drives out the spirits of the night.

—Oh, sing some more, Anastasia, please sing— Aleksei begged, bursting into tears. But Anastasia was already leaving the room in absolute silence, seeing no one, withdrawing to her sisters' room, shrouding herself in her white nightgown.

9

Almost all the soldiers in the regiment lost in Siberia were very young, and in any case were men who had been deprived of women for two years; they could talk of nothing else through those long July nights, and the names of wives and sweethearts left behind cast shadows of desire on the taiga from where came the echo of animals on the rampage—elks, sables, foxes, wolves, martens, ermines and, according to some, tigers.

At night the officers on sentry duty, passing among the tents on their tour of inspection, heard the sighs, sobs, murmurs and stifled laughter of those asleep, who dreamt what the officers themselves would dream when they came off duty, exhausted. Some stopped to listen in the darkness of the Siberian night to this ferment of sleeping life; it seemed to them that one and the same life-force was pulsating down there in the forest and here in the sleep of the soldiers, as if under the domed sky only one giant heart, the heart of the earth itself, were beating.

The devil is a woman . . . Prince Ypsilanti thought, dining with twenty of his officers who were telling him in an offhand way, making light of it, about the restlessness that possessed the regiment, the strange attitude that led to so many quarrels about nothing, the fits of nerves—as the regimental medical officer had smilingly defined it—that made the gentlest among them lose their tempers and the peaceable resort to violence. The prince, who was a man of the world, noticed that none of his officers ventured to go into the question of what effectively lay behind such phenomena. Since when could soldiers require the presence of women in a regiment and receive the backing of their officers? But these poor men were hardly soldiers anymore, since they'd been wandering around this accursed Siberia ... but that was no reason for him to find justification for them: everything had to appear as normal as usual.

—Gentlemen, let us think of more serious issues. The pleasure of having you at my table gives me also an opportunity to remind you that in a few weeks, at the end of the month, it will be the birthday of His Imperial Highness Tsarevich Aleksei Nicolaievich. As you well know Our Lord the Tsar has honored us by conferring on the heir to the throne the title of honorary colonel of the Preobrazhenskii, and we cannot let the day pass without celebration. If, as I believe, we shall soon be reaching our Tsar at Tobolsk ...— and here Ypsilanti's slow, deep voice rose, and his white-uniformed officers edged forward slightly, on impulse, watching their colonel, —I should like the Tsarevich to be our guest at the regimental dinner on that day, after parading the regiment and giving a demonstration of our excellent state of training despite the difficult circumstances. I've decided, therefore, that from tomorrow morning we will start a program of special drills, unit by unit, with a breakdown by specialization, to prepare for the parade of July thirtieth. We will train for a week, then split into two columns and set out. One will cross the taiga under the command of Khabalov, the other, under my command, will circle its western edge and join up at Tobolsk.—

Ypsilanti rose immediately to illustrate the plan on the map he had hung near the table, without giving anyone time to comment. His explanations, swift and concise as always, did not seem to admit questions, but as soon as he was silent it was clear he realized there would be some, for he walked slowly and heavily back to the table and poured himself a drink, looking deep into the bottom of the silver goblet. Khabalov was the first to speak:

—Your Excellency, I thank you for the great honor of giving me command of half the Preobrazhenskii. But how can you think of letting us pass through the taiga? You know full well that without expert guidance the taiga means death from fever, or from wild beasts.—

—Khabalov, in seventy-eight, when I was in charge of the thirty-seven men in my platoon, the Turks left us to enter the desert and gave us up for dead, but they did not take into account the endless patience of the Russian soldier and his adaptability. I'm still here and only three of the men died in crossing the desert. Don't you think that after what we've been through the taiga can hold no terrors for us? But perhaps you want to put another question to me: why don't I myself head the column crossing the taiga? I'm not afraid, believe me. I simply cannot allow myself to do it, I must absolutely reach the Tsar. I know I can count on your sense of honor and your readiness for sacrifice.—

—But, Your Excellency, no one knows where we are, who

we are, what's happening in the world . . . the war, the unrest in Petrograd, the Tsar at Tobolsk . . . can these things still be so?— Guderian was speaking, with his rolled French *r*'s, in an ironic tone that Ypsilanti did not miss.

—Perhaps things that should be true are no longer true for you, Guderian. This is not the first time you've shown yourself uncertain about something!—

—But will the soldiers be willing to obey us?—

Karel had risen, his eyes bloodshot and black-ringed, his voice on edge: he seemed ill. Rumor had it that he had recourse to the regimental doctor ever more frequently, and was relying heavily on drugs. But Ypsilanti respected his suffering, knew him to be completely trustworthy. The only worry was that he was young, too young to be in command. Perhaps he too, like the other young soldiers, shivered at night.

—Perhaps you were putting to yourself the question, whether you'd be able to obey?—

Ypsilanti had spoken in a whisper, conscious of the gravity of what he was implicitly admitting. And Karel shook, took a step toward the prince, flushed purple. He was immediately stopped by some other officers and collapsed in their arms in a faint. After an injection, he returned a little later to his place as if nothing had happened. In the meantime the conversation continued earnestly, mostly between officers rather than with the prince. He looked at them, turning his black eyes slowly from one to the other. But he didn't see them, he saw the soldier stripping to go, naked and happy, into the forest. It was that image that had stopped him from answering Karel more bluntly when he had raised the inopportune question of obedience. Because in fact the naked soldier fleeing into the taiga was no longer a poor madman, he was perhaps his entire

regiment and maybe something greater even than the Preobrazhenskii lost in Siberia. All Russia must at that moment be
lost and naked as the soldier who had refused to go on holding
a rifle. There must have been a good deal of truth to what
those damned Jews had said during the march to Vachitino.
Perhaps he was afraid of reaching Tobolsk, afraid to discover
the truth, perhaps he wanted to wander in the desert like the
Jews at the time of their biblical search for the Promised Land,
he wanted to die like Moses before reaching it. If there
no longer was a tsar, to whom could he, Prince Alexander
Ilarionovich Ypsilanti, offer his services? To whom could he
go to offer his intelligence and his experience? If happiness
lay in being the slave of a person or an ideology, if the most
profound anguish lay in belonging to no one, what life could
he have in a future outside the empire, in a Russia where men
were, like that soldier, naked and free, belonging to nobody,
reduced to hoboes in need of clothing, food, warmth, in a
world of hoboes subject to the same needs? He wanted to die
in the old Russia, and was preparing himself: the decision to
split the regiment was a mere consequence of such a purpose.
There was little time left if he wanted to salvage at least his
dignity in death.

—Gentlemen, please, a little silence! I think I have been
clear enough, and if there are no further objections, we shall
gather tomorrow at ten when I shall set out for you the detailed programs for the week. I hope you will want to join me
now in a toast to the health of the Emperor. . . .—

Getting up from the chair immediately pulled back by
Alyosha, he looked about him at those who had been his companions now for four years of the war. He saw some of them
hesitate, look at each other as though searching for an answer

to certain questions, then get up slowly until all were on their feet, and raising their glasses—some with empty glasses, others with glasses half-drained, like their faith.

—Refill Colonel Guderian's glass, and Major Stepanovich's, and the doctor's, and Captain Karel's ... their glasses seem to be empty,— the prince loudly ordered Alyosha. Who knows which one of them would be the first to betray, looting the reserves? And which one of them would never touch the provisions? He had to anticipate their moves, divide them, send the weakest into the taiga and keep with him the strongest, to lead them to death by a different way. This was why he had to split the regiment.

But the prince's plan was upset by an unexpected event. The following night a tiger managed to break through to the horses of the Saint George Squadron, and wrought havoc among those fine animals. Even Ypsilanti's white horse, Phaeton, had been killed—the prince himself had had to shoot him: he had reached him in time to see him wounded and bleeding after he had been woken by the clamor. The camp was in an indescribable turmoil. It was as if the tiger had brought with it a thousand devils and unleashed them, awakening all the aggressive instincts in those soldiers who had come to treat their rifle barrels as nothing more than a crutch during rest periods. They had spread out in squadrons, in platoons, in sections, along the whole border of the taiga, looking for the marauder. Some said they'd spotted her and followed her for a while. Others remembered with a shudder the yellow eyes as she disappeared into the thick undergrowth, but no one dared penetrate the forest. The horses agonized through the night, with cries that sounded almost human and brought tears to the eyes of those who heard them in their own way begging for death. The beast had killed three, but had wounded another ten in her attempts to feast upon warm fresh meat.

There was among the soldiers in the First Battalion a little Mongol who had barely talked to anyone: they regarded him as dumb, although they knew he was not. His task was to clean out the caldrons in the kitchen. That night he was among the first to rescue the horses, and he found his voice, explaining in a terrible Russian crammed with Asian dialects that it was the work of the "amba," as he called the tiger in his language, and that he could find her if they would follow him into the taiga, because he had been born in a Mongol village that bordered on a forest and the lake that was as big as a sea and he knew his way in there, especially at that time of the year, the season when he used to lay traps. They must not be afraid, the little Mongol told his commander, he knew his way in and out, just let them try him if they didn't believe him. And Kaigiar immediately proved the truth of what he had said: at midday he went into the forest with permission from his captain, carrying food in a bag, his rifle and a bow he unearthed from in front of his tent much to the astonishment of his companions. He promised to return by sunset, after giving three long elk calls. His commanding officer had let him tell of these customs, as he gazed at the trees at the forest's edge ... really the Imperial army was as vast and multifarious as Russia itself: Kaigiar, the silent, listless soldier they had been uncertain whether to consider dumb or an idiot, was now transformed into an ancient Asian hunter, familiar with those primitive rites and rituals of the hunt. Toward sunset the soldiers in Kaigiar's company could think of nothing else: would the little Mongol fellow return or would he too disappear as the crazed soldier had done? They stood around in silence, fearful of missing any sound that came from the taiga . . . and three long identical elk calls aroused excitement in hundreds of listening soldiers. It was the elk. It was genuinely the elk, that is, Kaigiar, cheerfully appearing over the horizon, a fact vouched for by three Yakuts who turned up at that very moment from their units, having recognized the beast's call which was imitated by hunters such as themselves in their home villages near the taiga of Lake Baikal. Kaigiar had never been so talkative: he carried his catch on his shoulders, some wonderful birds with long iridescent feathers like peacocks', an ermine and, trapped in a little cage, a small red vixen that yelped, showing her fangs. No one noticed that Ypsilanti was there too, hidden behind the crowd, listening with his men to the small Russian's mixed dialect, the sounds through which that strange and mysterious land at the tip of Russia spoke, where standards and swords counted only for defense or for hunting, never as symbols of a faith. Did danger or help come from that quarter? But the thought of his dear Phaeton torn apart in the jaws of the tiger, the memory of those eyes as the colonel loaded his revolver to shoot the animal restored his self-assurance, and he made his way through the throng.

—And "amba"? Where will "amba" be now? Can you capture her? A hundred silver rubles if you bring back her skin, Private Kaigiar.—

Kaigiar's expression had changed as soon as he noticed the white oblong head of Ypsilanti above that of the soldiers; he had let the little cage drop at his feet and stood to attention, but stood badly, all crooked and twisted as if someone had surprised him doing something he shouldn't. And he had fallen silent again, as he had been before the tiger came out of the taiga. Ypsilanti had to repeat the question, helped by the three hunters from southern Yakutia who knew Kaigiar's dialect. It took time before the Mongol understood and got over his terror of the colonel, who was about to leave, tired of that idiot who could not understand. Yes, Kaigiar agreed to capture the tiger, even though it would be difficult because she was a tiger of a rare species, exceptionally ferocious, able to run through the taiga as swift as the wind, appearing and vanishing here and there, at great distances, as if capable of multiplying herself. But he knew, like all good hunters, that there was only one, he would never let himself be fooled. However, he did not feel like going on his own, Ypsilanti had to give him at least ten men as good as himself.

—And where are we going to find them? We've only got three,— the prince answered irritably. But Kaigiar nodded, yes, if the colonel ordered it, he was well able to find more than half a dozen men who were up to hunting in the taiga. And within two days not six but twenty men from different units, who did not know each other, were flushed out by the little Mongol. He had noticed them in the mess, in the infirmary, as they marched during exercises, on horseback when they fired their weapons. He had recognized them even if he did not know their names or their ranks, by the way they moved their hands when they cut wood with their knives, the way they crawled so as not to be seen by the enemy, the way they sniffed the air during drills, how they rubbed away their footprints, how they could call to each other imitating the calls of animals he had seen so frequently, how they covered their urine. He knew from all those details that they were hunters like himself.

The fierce apparition of the tiger—even though in fact no one had actually seen it—and the presence among them concealed in the uniform of the Preobrazhenskii, of Kaigiar, the Yakuts and all those hunters who for days told their companions of their adventures and achievements, was slowly changing the feelings of many toward the taiga: they began to see it now not as an enchanted forest, but as a place through which they could actually walk, eat, sleep, encounter adventures that no one who had never been in there could imagine. The taiga held unforeseeable surprises, like the time that Kaigiar came across a village so primitive it seemed inconceivable it could exist in the Russia of the twentieth century. He had been treated like a beautiful, fearsome animal, just as they regarded the tiger, and had been given food and gifts so long as he went away, left them alone, especially the women whom they kept isolated in huts on the edge of the village.

Ypsilanti noticed everything. The work of that week distracted the troops from the absurdity of their situation, and the tiger and the hunters like Kaigiar made possible what had seemed before the dream of crazed suicide, the penetration of the taiga to reach Tobolsk; as long as the soldiers of the forest kept on wearing the uniform of the army of His Imperial Majesty the Tsar of all the Russias. And Russia was indeed many, one could vanish into one of its many parts and still be within the empire, as Kaigiar had been within the army, though silent. Ypsilanti let them organize beats in the forest, so that a great number of the soldiers got used to it ... until he should decide who would go with him and who follow Khabalov. As he anticipated, such adventurous curiosity spread through the soldiers that Ypsilanti had to keep his promise to Kaigiar and let him organize the tiger hunt.

10

Someone had ransacked the basement at Ipatiev's: suit-cases and trunks lay open, their contents spilled and plundered. The childish larcenists had taken all nonessentials, apart from the boots, things that no one who did not belong to the Imperial family would be able to wear, the richest fabrics, the girls' evening gowns, brooches, boots, the Tsar's hunting spurs, ceremonial uniforms, sashes, dressing gowns, the Tsaritsa's wide-brimmed hats. Nicholas smiled, thinking that some soldier—for it had certainly been the soldiers who had done the looting—must have tried to get his mother into Olga's evening wear or Alice's hats, those large showy white hats for which she and her older sister Elizabeth, Uncle Sergei's widow, were famous in all the courts of Europe.

There had always been a certain rivalry between Alice and Elizabeth, similar to that between Dagmar, their mother, and the Queen of England, Alexandra. Elizabeth exuded an exhilarating energy that bereavement tested but never consumed. Her face stopped the years in their tracks, and they circled her like performers in a dance, never attacking. She knew how to live: she could lie so well to herself she forgot she was inventing half her life. The other half belonged to the Tsar's sister-in-law, the Imperial grand duchess, widow of Sergei, mother of two daughters, an exemplar of modesty and religious piety. But Nicholas loved the lying, spirited, ageless Elizabeth, the mistress of Uncle Aleksei, a married brother of the Grand Duke Sergei; although in the know, Nicholas had always feigned ignorance of the relationship, and they had spent hours discussing Uncle Aleksei without acknowledging to each other what Nicholas knew. In time, as they talked about Grand Duke Aleksei, he took on the shape of the ideal man, his was the sort of love Nicholas would dream of—but was it only men like his uncle who could thus be loved? He thought love was what others felt, something he himself had to learn, as if it were an art he was uncertain he would ever understand. He was greatly saddened when some relative's marriage failed and he, as head of the Imperial household, had to give permission for the divorce, not for moral reasons, but because he had invariably believed the "forever" that formed the basis of the marriage vows. He knew that his own marriage was a liturgical act, the rite of a monarch, rather than a bond of love.

One day he had gone to see Elizabeth at her daughter's house outside Moscow, on the hill of sparrows. He had found her up a cherry tree, barefoot, throwing fruit into her daughter's apron: Alice called her "the wild one." When she saw the Emperor, she leaped from the tree with the ease and grace of a girl.

—Would you like some cherries, Your Imperial Majesty?— she had laughed, dropping into a deep curtsy. Beatrice stood by, looking at her mother, profoundly embarrassed. That time, throughout the return journey to Moscow, he had wondered what it would have been like to have lived with her. Now, looking down at Aleksei on the swing Trup and Kharitonov had built in the garden, he remembered the Aleksei loved by his sister-in-law, whom he had envied so much. He had always seemed the most colorless of his father's brothers: how did he have the luck to be loved by such a woman? He had not even been faithful, he neglected her for cheap trollops, as Nicholas knew from confidential police reports. How could Elizabeth not have seen how empty-headed and superficial he was. But he remembered what she had said once, which only gradually he had learned to understand:

—Give me only a little of a man, a very little, I'll make up the rest. . . .—

Down in the garden Aleksei had relinquished the swing; Nicholas did not want to lose sight of him. He saw him start a game that needed no witnesses and went down to support him, to draw the attention of the doctor and the attendant away from him. The game was the journeys of Aleksei, precisely routed, through Italy, France, England and, God only knew why, to Iceland. Ipatiev's iron benches were transformed into the most beautiful cities of Europe. The shady, isolated, northern footpath to the pomegranate tree was Iceland, that cold Atlantic island. France was the area of the gates, and Aleksei, moving toward the forbidden exit, thought they should go to France more frequently. "Now though I must return to my Iceland," he then said to himself, looking around to make sure no one was observing him. And he started on the longest journey, the one from which he always had to be called back, toward the pomegranate, the northern footpath. "Now we're in Reykjavík, where there is no king and the King of Denmark never comes because it's too cold, and there are only the highest mountains and volcanoes. If I didn't remember you, who would ever come? Because I know it, one day the spell will break and you will wake, my beautiful sleeping island. I know you need me, you need me to believe that you are the most powerful, the greatest, the most beautiful. I'll marry you because anyway, he, my uncle, the King of Denmark, he won't care, he won't even notice. . . ." Aleksei would sit on the ground and start singing, sketching with a stone on the earth the face of his island, the face of a girl who followed him with hesitant, troubled steps, as though unaware of him waiting for her ahead, as if not seeing him. Her hands were shut like unopened flowers, and her hair was loose. Only the colors were missing; the boy could not give color by sketching with a stone on the ground. But Aleksei would immediately rub out the drawing and start again, humming. Sometimes he would crossly throw away the stone he was using and look for a softer one, or a harder one, and he might use his fingers when some detail did not come out as he wanted it to. If he found himself sketching one of his sisters, he would become angry and blush.

—It's not like that, it's not like that,— he would repeat, and would start it again.

—Nicholas, I think Aleksei talks to himself,— Alice remarked. —At least in Tobolsk he played with the soldiers, but here he talks to himself.—

—He's a child, he's not even fourteen, let him play as he wants, it's all right,— Nicholas answered. It seemed natural to him: in fact he would have liked to know what games he played, what ghosts he saw in the garden. One day the boy came and asked him where on earth were the Falkland Islands: he had read of their existence in an English newspaper of the doctor's. Nicholas told him they were in the South Atlantic, that they had some thousand inhabitants and an English governor.

—Oh, but not those islands, you're wrong. They have such a beautiful name. . . .— And he added them to his itineraries in the garden.

One morning the Imperial family was woken by the songs of soldiers on guard: obscene songs about the Tsaritsa and the grand duchesses. Nicholas rapidly gathered his family and the retinue and, opening the prayer book that had once belonged to his father, began very loudly to sing the hymn to the Redeemer that they had so often sung together on Easter Day. Olga, then Tatiana, Maria, Anastasia, Aleksei, Demidova, Kharitonov, Trup, Leonid the scullery boy, the doctor and finally even Alice joined in. And they were still singing when Jurovsky burst in like thunder, shouting to stop it. Nicholas lashed out, invoking the International Red Cross agreement regarding political prisoners, but was immediately sorry he had given the man that much recognition of power. He had listened to Alice and felt he had lost a battle. I don't know how to negotiate or to defend myself. I've never in my life had to do it and I will certainly not learn now. I started to sing a hymn, and that stopped them.

That day he was thinking of the death penalties meted out in his name, the name of the Tsar of all the Russias, Nicholas II; but none weighed on his conscience, for none did he feel remorse: they were acts of power, with a reprieve in one hand and condemnation in the other, like the great fresco by Michelangelo in Rome, the city he would have liked to see on his journey to Italy but which, because of Italian internal politics, he had not been able to visit in October 1909. As a boy, his tutors had explained to him that it was there, beneath that naked Christ who separated the good from the bad, that the Europeans, through the grace of the Holy Spirit, chose their last absolute monarch, the Catholic Pope. He would have liked to talk to the Pope, to understand why southern Europe should have wanted to relegate power, which is the sacred in its most human manifestation, to life after death. He would have liked to ask him to unravel the knot of contradiction that originated in those countries where his pontifical word reached: why admit Christ's gesture, the hand raised to separate the good from the bad, in the afterlife, and only in the afterlife, and foster a pretense, here on earth, confusing the simple values of eternity with those of history? The Catholic religion was too merciful and would perish at the hands of the democracies that enjoyed its blessing.

He had always been fascinated by a figure from *The Last Judgment* by Michelangelo: one of the damned on the left of Christ (and each time he thought of it Nicholas would, for a fraction of a second, forget which was right and which was left) just below Saint Bartholomew displaying the empty rag of his skin; the figure cowered, covering one eye with his hand. In none of the Russian icons had Nicholas ever seen such an expression in the eye of the damned. In Russia the damned were not taken by surprise, they were convinced of their damnation from childhood; perhaps they had even been prepared for it by him, by the Tsar. In Europe, in Rome, however, that black, wild look, that vision of an eternity between two blinks of an eyelid, could only manifest itself within a soul who had never heard of God. No one on earth had prepared that soul for judgment; all the kings anointed by the Pope had lied.

Cicadas were singing of the greatness of Russia that afternoon in July, and Nicholas thought of all the cicadas in the empire, the energy of all those songs sung before and after the revolution by those who did not know on what tree they were perched, to what regime they belonged; he felt he himself had almost forgotten who he was, and that he too would be able to stop singing soon, as soon as the sun allowed. Because it was the sun that compelled cicadas to sing, and the cicadas awoke the sun at daybreak. He felt he might be becoming one of those invisible cantors, able to sleep one night before starting a new song. But what man had ever turned into a cicada? Alice drew near and sat next to him. They were alone.

—What were you thinking, Nicholas? You looked so far away . . . what were you thinking?—

—I was thinking of Rome. You remember that visit to Italy, the demonstration against us that prevented us from visiting Rome? And I was thinking of cicadas. Can't you hear them singing? And of so many other things, my dear. . . .—

—You have time to think of cicadas? I'm so tired, Nicholas, so tired that sometimes I just want to lie down and sleep and never wake up. If it wasn't for the children–I think I've lived long enough.—

—No, Alice, it's not over yet. Maybe it never is. . . .—

—What do you mean? . . .—

—Oh, nothing. I was thinking of the cicadas. . . .—

—Tomorrow the priest comes; that tyrant has given permission again. I'd hoped the man would let him come on Tuesday, for Saint Aleksei, but it has to be tomorrow. Perhaps I'll learn something of the Whites. Gilliard must still be in town–the priest might ferret him out and give him a message for the Whites. Let's just hope this priest is braver–the last one turned out to be so untrustworthy. I've drawn up a plan of the house and the garden, it could be useful if they attack us, don't you think?— And she showed him a pencil drawing of the inside of the house. She was still talking about it late into the night.

It was hot that night. How difficult it is to sleep tonight, Aleksei was thinking. Cats in heat were keeping many awake. Dimitri, the guard on duty at the door to the apartment, did not know how to make the time pass and strode up and down, then leaned out of the open landing window to look into the dark. Another hour and a half to go. He could hear the grand duchesses talking in their room. He thought he recognized Maria's voice, the most mature of the four voices. The cats in the garden had so much to tell each other it was no use throwing stones as Kharitonov was doing: a couple of minutes and they were at it again. Dimitri could hear beyond them; he could hear the chickens, the pigeons, the ducks and the puppies at home in the Ukraine. But were these cats or souls in purgatory?

Kharitonov could not sleep. He heard the cats as the dead, demanding to be remembered by the living, and shuddered each time the wails reached a certain pitch and seemed to call his name, Piotr Kharitonov, Piiioootr Khariiitooonov—his name, inherited from his grandfather.

—Listen, listen to them.—

—Come on, go to sleep, you fool. You can't be frightened of a couple of cats,— Trup, the sleepy attendant, answered, turning over on his side.

Dimitri listened to Maria's voice, half-closing his eyes, stretching out against the wall. My God how can I stay here alone, how can I go on waiting for that idiot Ivan. . . . He thought Maria knew he was outside, that she raised her voice on purpose. As it was, during their walks, when it was his turn to accompany them, she was always by his side, and looked straight at him over the others' heads, with a look he found difficult to sustain. What fault was it of his if he had to guard them? If he was a soldier and she a daughter of Nicholas Romanov? He had asked to be transferred, he did not like being a jailer. He had asked, but Jurovsky had not wanted to know.

—It'll only be a little while longer anyway, Comrade Dimitri,— he had finished by saying, raising his eyes to the second-floor windows. Who knows, perhaps they'll take them away again, Dimitri had thought; they'll never get away from here. But one night he had dreamt there was no one in the house commandeered from the engineer Ipatiev. He had woken with a great thirst, and had got up to go and look for them, but had stopped himself after a few steps. . . . What am I doing, going to check on them? They're in there sleeping. It's Aleksei's watch now. And he had returned to bed after getting a drink. —Those cats, is there no way to shut them up?—

Alice whispered in her room, but Nicholas was in Livadia, could not hear her. He was dreaming, dreaming of talking to his father of the decision to be taken, to close Crimea to the revolutionaries and reclaim the sea, make it a land into which to expand. Fish came to shore, raised their heads on the beach and called: —Nicholas, Nicholas, don't listen to your father, don't listen.— But Alexander III insisted: —Remember to take the most faithful divisions south, my son. It's easy to close off the Crimea. I must go by sea, you can reclaim it once I've gone; my ship will be the last, then you will reign over all the land under the sea.—

Alice had silently drawn near to Aleksei's bed.

—Mother, don't let's wake Father, he's asleep.—

—You can't sleep because of the cats either?—

—What must they feel to make such human wails?—

—They're ill, Aleksei. But now, try and sleep.— Alice left the room, met Dimitri's eye. She can't sleep either, thought the soldier. And after she had gone into her daughters' room he could no longer hear Maria's voice.

—Olga, are you still awake? Aleksei is too, but your father is asleep. Remember the priest comes tomorrow; let's hope he can do something for us.—

—Don't hope, Mother; he'll be a poor creature like the other,— Olga answered.

Demidova stood by the window in her room. Kharitonov had only just calmed down, and she was still smiling. She was not afraid of the dead; she was afraid of those soldiers' faces, young men who came from the Ural Soviet, and had only recently joined. Such different types from those of Tsarskoe Selo and Tobolsk. . . . She could have gone, been free, she did not belong to the Imperial family, but it would never cross her mind, she would follow them anywhere. Who would look after her mistress, the Tsaritsa who had found a place for her sick brother in the seminary in Moscow, and for her other brother, Andrei, a position in the Imperial Civil Service? They owed everything to the Tsaritsa, and they were not people who forget a favor. It does not matter where one's daily bread comes from, as she would have liked to explain to Avadeyev, the jailer before Jurovsky, who had sneeringly tagged her, along with Trup and Kharitonov, as "bootlickers of those assassins." The scoundrel had stolen: one day a pair of shoes, another a coat, another a pen belonging to the Tsarevich, poor boy; a mere sneak thief, that's all he was. Oh, how topsy-turvy the world is. I wonder where Father and my brothers are now? thought Demidova. It was the only thing that was really painful, not having news of her family and of Nina, her little niece, who had just started to walk when they left for Siberia on that train guarded by machine guns at the front and the back. Nina was now beyond those black mountains and certainly by now had learned to speak, perhaps they had taught her her aunt's name ... she was like those kittens, her little Nina was, when she held her. Damn the revolution, damn the war, what have they got to do with my Nina, or with me? And the Tsaritsa's most faithful maid wiped her eyes with the corner of her apron, looking up at the stars.

Joy, Aleksei's spaniel, gamboled around her, wagging his eager tail.

—You heard the cats, eh, Joy? Or did you hear me crying? You poor thing, you too, I've nothing to give you to eat.— And she took him in her arms, thinking of Nina.

11

The soldiers of His Imperial Majesty did not know there was no tsar in Russia; they ran through the taiga behind Kaigiar the Mongol, who spoke no Russian but understood the language of wolves, elks, partridges. In the course of their forays they had been trained to speak as little as possible, though they could not yet leap as Kaigiar could—he would vanish like one of the spirits he feared and tried to conciliate.

Sometimes they thought he was only a few steps away, they felt his presence in the tangle of undergrowth and branches; the call of the capercaillie would startle them, make them look up, and there was Kaigiar, who had climbed high to see farther, as far as he could in that sea of green. Some of the more athletic, like Ignatic the Georgian, had been tempted and had climbed to the top of the tallest tree. When he reached the top he was so struck by what he saw he forgot the hunt. Wherever he turned his gaze there was a vast expanse of different greens against a sky of the most intense blue he had ever seen. The tops were not level: some, braver, prouder, seemed to want to burst through the sky, hardly content with their height, merely pausing until the following spring in their dream of touching the clouds. Other areas of the forest were more rounded, more welcoming, seemed more concerned to furnish perches and hiding places; they were bursting with the life to be found in the nests and in the burrows under the tree roots. They were obviously older trees, more ancient than the ones whose tips pointed brazenly to the sky; perhaps they had reached those blue heights the younger ones aspired to and had forgotten about them, letting themselves be absorbed by the lives they sheltered. Up there, Ignatic thought that, really, hours, days, years, were all the same and there was no sense in counting them. Some broad-winged birds in the distance plunged with the speed of predators, and a high strident call told him that one life had been sacrificed for another according to the oldest laws on earth, the law of the strongest, and he remembered the tiger, the "amba" who had devoured a haunch of his commander's horse. From below came the calls of his companions who had noticed his absence.

—Ignatic, Ignatic . . .— It was pleasant to hear his name, to look out over the endless plain and hear the warmth of those familiar voices. It was enough to make one want to lose one's bearings, to make one forget the war, the regiment, the Tsar, the call of his companions, Misha's teasing, his faraway village. Slowly he climbed back down, and appeared a few minutes later in front of a terrified Misha and the rest of the platoon.

—Are you mad, Ignatic? A couple more minutes and we would have lost you. You're a far cry from the Mongol. If you'd got lost you'd have ended up like the poor crazy Piotr Ivanovich. . . .— Misha was beside himself, but within half an hour was teasing again.

—What do you think, Ignatic, that you have wings like an

angel? He wanted to fly to his beautiful Matrojana, didn't you, Ignatic?— And his companions teased him and tormented him until they reached the great river where Kaigiar had advised the captain they should stop to rest and eat.

—What river is it?— the captain asked Kaigiar. The soldier looked at him without answering: he seemed amused. One of the Yakuts answered for him.

—He says the river is river, sir. He doesn't know what it's called, you must bear with him.—

But if he didn't know its name, Kaigiar clearly knew its currents, its shallows, its temperature, its fish, the rapids, as no geographer of the Military Geographical Institute in St. Petersburg knew them who had drawn the thin blue line on the map of Siberia. He crouched in a recess of the shore and a few minutes later caught a striped red-and-green fish. Kaigiar ate slowly, picking those parts of the fish and the preserved meat that would give him greatest stamina, drank a lot, each time wiping his face and hands with vodka, careless of his clothes. He listened to no reason when it came to putting out the fire they had used to roast the birds and the fish: fire was sacred and could be of use to others in the taiga. When the soldiers understood that he claimed the fire could be used by others, they smiled. Who else was there, in that boundless forest? Unless they were to believe the tales with which Kaigiar had entertained them some nights before around the campfire. . . .

—Amba, amba! . . .— Kaigiar stopped and made a sign to be quiet. He seemed a different person, no longer the small, plump, comic-looking Mongol, but a severe and unsettling statue, his look directed not outward to an object glimpsed at out there through the trees, but inward, as if in the end the beast were to be found within himself. He was quickly able to communicate by gesture, with no words, what each man should do, spread in a formation through the taiga. A movement started in the thick of the forest that many thought just illusion, as if the hunters who kept each group linked up with Kaigiar deceived with their calls not only the tiger, who had shown herself like a golden streak to Misha and Ignatic, but all the members of the expedition. The most uneasy was the captain who had asked the name of the river. Thinking of his responsibility in face of the colonel, aware that in any case they had to be back at the camp within two days, he asked himself after a few hours of pursuit whether it was not better to use his authority and call back Private Kaigiar. But Private Kaigiar was no longer there; he had made himself as invisible as the tiger. And just as Kaigiar had sensed the tiger without seeing her, so the soldiers and the hunters sensed Kaigiar, though they could no longer see him. He had taken to moving aboveground, from branch to branch, as if he no longer wanted to touch the earth where smells, footprints, the sound of breaking branches, the displacing of stones, the crushing of leaves underfoot, could alert the tiger.

He tried to move as she did, to speak her language in a kind of courtship, and the gray of his uniform could barely be seen against the green. But high up, the blue of the sky was darkening, the sunset was drawing near, the light was fading. Could he still continue in pursuit? The captain was about to recall Kaigiar with his whistle, when one shot, then a second, resounded dryly. A bloodcurdling roar, then silence.

Everyone freezes. A strange, incredible cry is heard, a long-drawn-out musical wail which modulates into a kind of rhythmic, monotonous primitive chant. Kaigiar is voicing his joy

and thanking the gods, offering them the victim. A few minutes later the fifty men of the expedition are gathered around
Kaigiar who does not even see them until he has finished his
incantation. Then he reverts to being a soldier in the Fourth
Company, First Battalion, turns to the captain, shows him the
dead tiger. The hunters look at him with admiration and a
touch of envy; they would have liked to track down their
quarry themselves. . . . The soldiers stand around the captain,
who touches the head of the tiger: a trickle of blood seeps out
just above the yellow staring eyes. No doubt about it, Kaigiar
has been magnificent. What rejoicing there will be back at the
camp when they bring in the quarry! Ignatic cannot resist a
moment's feeling of unease in front of that spent force, a kind
of strange sympathy for what until a few minutes before has
been a solitary and free life. He thinks, already ten minutes
have passed since its death, and for that wonderful free beast
the captivity of eternity has begun in no less a way than for
the more humble animals, prisoners of man, like cats, dogs,
chickens, once they die. Now the colonel's horse has been
avenged. Misha comes near.

—Isn't she a splendid beast though, eh, Ignatic? Look, she
seems still ready to maul, look at those fangs, look at those
muscles. It's easy to see how she could have attacked all those
horses, eh? And we, we saw her only moments before, streak-
ing past, unreachable. . . .—

Ah, yes, they had been the last to see her alive. Kaigiar
turned at that, catching the words, and seemed afraid, looked
at them as if they might be in danger, as if there was something he wasn't sure he should tell them. He preferred to
speak in his dialect to one of the hunters while Ignatic and
Misha looked at each other, perplexed. The thing was, the

hunter explained after Kaigiar had finished, that the Mongol
was superstitious like all his race, and according to them,
whoever sees a live tiger last and does not pray, offering the
dead beast to the gods, has the evil eye on him and gets lost
in the taiga. Kaigiar kept on looking at the two Russian soldiers, apprehensively, but the night bivouac was being orga-
nized, the first night in the taiga without its tiger. Misha, who
lacked all respect for the gods of the forest, knew immediately
how to react to Kaigiar's ill omen:

—Ah, but we're not afraid of the evil eye, are we, Ignatic?
Ypsilanti is there to drive it away. He's got a worse curse than
any in the taiga and we are under his dominion, we are invul-
nerable because of it. . . .— And while he laughed he remembered the crazy soldier who had said the very same thing.

Only Kaigiar and the hunters managed to sleep that night;
time and again the other soldiers made to snatch up their
rifles: the forest seemed dead during the day by comparison,
and even the tents of the encampment on the plain in front of
the taiga, those tents they had cursed so often during the long
march, were preferable to this night in the open. And yet they
had been homeless for years now, and had practically forgotten what a brick house with windows and doors was like. Only
Ignatic had not lost the sense of peace he had experienced up
in the tree gazing at the boundless view, and seemed to wait
trustingly in the dark, certain he would return up there at the
break of day. And light broke through, as Ignatic believed it
would: not the light of a common day, such as they saw each
morning as the flag was raised, the standard with the black
Imperial eagle on a red ground. This was a slow heavy light,
warm as a blanket, crackling like newly baked bread. It
seemed to follow an inverse path, arriving from every direc-

tion, from the grass, from the branches, from the stones, and took possession of those half-slumbering men who had only now managed to escape from the taiga into their dreams. It traveled up along the trunks and the leaves and finally reached the tips and settled regally in the sky.

Kaigiar woke, opening his eyes abruptly like an animal on its guard. He had heard a snake in his sleep, and he was right, a snake close to the captain was shot by a soldier. Now the tiger seemed somehow more firmly dead, now that another danger had been avoided, as if the snake had succeeded in relegating the tiger further back in time. Kaigiar would have to skin it, to bring it back to the regiment, and went in search of the herbs he needed. The soldiers, exhausted by a sleepless night, spread out toward the river to wash.

Ignatic looked for his tree along the bank of that river on which it was impossible to imagine any boat leaving a wake. But he could not decide which one he should climb and kept on walking, looking up and tripping frequently over roots. He stopped to drink, lying on the ground and leaning his chest on the bank with his head over the water. He looked into the water but didn't see his face reflected in the trembling surface. Instead he saw a dark gentle face with large shining yellow eyes. He hesitated a moment to look up, perhaps that mirror lied; fear held him still, looking into the water, hoping to see only his pale face. But a feminine voice speaking a strange language reached him. He turned and saw a young woman clothed only by her long hair. He was ashamed of being dressed, lowered his eyes. The woman smiled at him and started a long speech with a voice more tender than that of a child. The word "amba" recurred more often than any other and reflected in her face and wondering eyes a blend of joy and terror, as if she wanted to communicate to him something like gratitude. She kept on pointing vaguely into the taiga, then touching his hand, and stooping to brush it with her lips. When she finally grasped it as if to take him with her, Ignatic shook himself and found his voice:

—Who are you? Do you speak Russian? I can't come with you, I have to go back to my comrades.—

He was more ashamed of his words than of his clothes, they struck him as indecent, as if they had tainted the river, the trees, the blue sky forevermore. Why ever had he spoken? And she too seemed sad, as if she had been rejected and humiliated. She looked at herself as if she were ashamed of something, as if she were suddenly aware of being naked, and repeated the only sound she had grasped: —Comrades? . . . Comrades? . . .— and remained in suspense, raising questioning eyes to Ignatic, who would have given much not to have spoken, not to see the smile with which she had first greeted him vanish from her lips. But he felt also that on those lips the word lost its everyday meaning, and the months fell away, fled, the years of war, vanquished by a word so bound up with death and imprisonment. He burst out laughing, as if a vast joy had suddenly raised him high up in the tree from which the morning before he had looked long into the boundless land that did not know its name, where the young woman was using up one by one the few remaining hours before she met him.

He took her hand and brought it to his laughing lips. And now the smile returned to her face and she again made the gesture that he should go with her. And slowly Ignatic followed her.

12

Alice, don't turn on the light, I beg you, leave me, leave me alone by the light of the streetlamps.— Alice had come back into the room and found Nicholas awake in the semidarkness.

Nicholas watched the ceiling, counting the shadows of the rare passersby: five so far, all nameless, but he knew there were five. He was making their acquaintance, as one does meeting someone along the way, the kind of acquaintance that can lead to friendship but probably will not, after the usual small talk about the weather, the destination and the reason for the journey. But now, he remembered he had never traveled, he had never been the stranger who gradually reveals himself by the way he offers a cigarette, crosses his legs, gets up to close the train window. No, he had never been a Ulysses dressed in rags who turns up and suddenly the entire household, men and women, sense he has returned. No, wherever he had gone, he had been immediately, blindingly, the greatest a man could be, the Tsar. He had not let the faint light from outside reach him, had not let the eyes of his companions grow used to his face in the semidarkness, while the train cut through the night, and only the occasional station light ran across his features without revealing him completely. What did he know of journeys, in the end? His compartment had always been fully lit across plains and through tunnels, along coasts and in stations. The Tsar's blue train never traveled in darkness, the Tsar could never be in the dark, everyone had to be able to see him. And he must not see them, merely know that their eyes were on him. Everywhere in the empire it was the same hour, the same light, because the empire was that train that traveled in full light day or night. Heaven help them if the Tsar were to be plunged in darkness, if the engineers forgot to switch on the lights in a tunnel. What would happen to their god in the dark, a god who belonged to no one, who let himself be touched and recognized in the semblance of a man, forgetting his own name? What did this fear suggest, this terror of plunging into darkness, not being able to recognize north and south, height and depth, left and right? Where did the darkness lead to? If only it did lead to some place. Was this movement merely apparent, and would this be seen clearly when the illusion of light failed?

"Have courage, Nicholas. Have courage to be afraid." He thought he heard someone encouraging him finally to be afraid, be fearful of so much darkness, not to be apprehensive of falling into the darkness, as though it were like the trick at the fair he had attended as a boy where it seems as if the drop is meters deep and it is merely twenty centimeters.

The next day light was everywhere, and Nicholas felt it was a reward, that light that invaded Ipatiev's house after his night. Alice, who managed to thread a needle without glasses, looked at him gratefully. No one could escape the brilliance, no corner of the house was spared, dust showed its gold everywhere.

The rays through the shutters seemed to Aleksei like the rays that shone out of the great eye of God in icons. For the women the light induced a desire to sweep, wash floors, do something to deserve it and enhance its brilliance, and for the men there was a new pleasure in doing whatever it was they were doing, without thinking ahead, but living for the moment, content within its bounds, not wishing to escape it. The soldiers took their turns on guard, Jurovsky applied himself to his plan for death, the cook to his steaks, the doctor to Aleksei's sedatives. The miracle of the great light was that everything was happening as if nothing would ever change. What's the matter with them, they seem electrified ... Jurovsky asked himself, watching the Romanovs and their entourage.

It seemed as if time wanted a pause to rest: Tatiana kept on looking at her watch and it seemed always eleven. Could it be that the activity of the women was dictated by fear that time would stand still, that the light was like a blind man's, living a life of which sighted people knew nothing? Perhaps the women wanted to help the day along, beating time with their work to move the stunned hours. Nicholas walked and felt the muscles of his legs, the rhythm of his breathing, the pulsing of his blood. Everything was finally contained in the three or four activities of the day; there was no need to think beyond what engaged him: to give his children their lessons, read the Bible aloud, take a walk in the garden, join the doctor in checking the effect of the medicines on Aleksei, write his diary, pray with his family, eat his meals.

But if that light was time that had clotted and coagulated, it was as cold as a new wisdom. To see and understand now seemed to Nicholas tantamount to abandoning all interest in the few things that occupied his day. The anxiety that had been his enduring companion was a guarantee that he suffered in Ekaterinburg every hour from his constant hope to be gone, to save himself and his family. This fantasy was warm, full of love of life, though it carried lies and anxiety in its wake. Now the chess set of their nights and days was even more intensely black and white, and it seemed to Nicholas that their days were flashing by, rushing headlong between darkness and light, light and darkness, unstoppably. An adventure had started that reminded him of his brother Mikhail, the only member of the family able to forget he was a Romanov.

—When will you make up your mind to come with me, Nicholas, to disguise yourself as a merchant and board the next train? You'll see who you'll meet. Imagine what a wonderful experience for one of *us* to be nobody anymore!— Nicholas had always thought that brother of his bizarre, acting as if he believed so little in his own role, with his frequent escapades to the West. But of all his relatives, he was the one Nicholas would have most liked to see again. He had lived abroad for years; whenever he returned to Russia he preferred the company of servants on whom he bestowed the gift of his desperate royalty. He rejected the company of his equals, especially his family. At Orel he could be found in the stables of the estate, with an eternal glass of champagne in his hand, laughing and joking with the cooks and stable lads, frequently in competition with them in an intimacy that had nothing egalitarian or democratic about it. The largest of Mikhail Romanov's cooks, wearing his master's rings on the first joints of his thick fingers, seemed to act as custodian of that Garden of Eden where everyone was first, without any imposition of supremacy. If the grand duke judged that his servant was sincerely loyal, he would confront the man with terrifying requests. He might say to him that if he had any gratitude, he had to help save him from a horrible death, he must kill him immediately:

—There, shoot me, help me if you love me!— he would say, handing over his revolver.

The brother of the Tsar had returned from one of his visits abroad married to a divorced Moscow woman. When they met after the wedding, Mikhail had let his brother run on with his reproaches about a decision so counter to the interests of the dynasty. Then, leaning toward him and looking him straight in the eye, he said:

—Nicholas, you've never seen her, or you'd understand. If you had come with me on the journey like an ordinary Russian, you would understand. . . .— Those who had seen Natalia Serementov, the morganatic wife of Mikhail, all agreed with the French ambassador's opinion that she was "the most beautiful woman in Russia." When she appeared on the streets of Moscow with her light graceful stride, Paléologue had said, all the men straightened their ties and walked more erect, wanted her to like them, to be considered attractive.

He had abdicated in favor of Mikhail, not only because he was the only other surviving son of Alexander III; it had been the most desperate concession, the final throw—opening the way to a constitutional monarchy, because Mikhail could have been this new kind of tsar. But Mikhail was dead, and Nicholas did not know it. Not even Natalia, not even love had saved him; he was always a Romanov, the younger brother of the Tsar. The world was an exile from the Garden of Eden, and the world could not forgive the race of fallen angels, now that it had taken possession of its frontiers. But Nicholas knew that the same uncertain frontiers of his spirit that had let the revolution through, were also a sign of a different orbit, of a new world to which God had destined a new dynasty. Much better to sleep with the old Russia that was now sinking. There was no question of keeping the reality of his country in one form only. He thought it had fallen to him to help the disease discharge its poison, polluting the cicadas, the summers, the sun. There was the Russia of nature and the Russia of history, and he was Tsar of the former. With the Russia of history he had nothing more to do, it was beyond him, beyond the windows and the garden.

He looked at his watch: it was three o'clock in the afternoon according to all the clocks in the empire, but he knew that was not so, that to give his subjects a common time, many different hours had to be harmonized. On journeys to any province in the empire, before telling the Sovereign the hour, the big slow hours of the East had to mesh with the small fast hours of the West, and, if he was going to Poland, he would learn after a few minutes the time to follow until he reached Warsaw, and if he was going to Siberia, the hour which would serve until Vladivostok.

Nicholas looked at a glass forgotten by Demidova on the windowsill. That object, separated from its kind, far from the rest of the tableware, was like himself. And yet what other associations there were in that glass that gave drink to the wind ... it was still wet from the wine. Who had drunk from it? The Tsaritsa or the air, jealous of all that crimson? I'm going mad, Nicholas told himself when he noticed Dr. Botkin, I'm talking to glasses. He rose to go in to Aleksei with Olga and Maria.

—Tomorrow it will rain,— Maria said from the window.

—See the heat lightning in the air this evening, how unsettled the weather is.—

—No, Maria; the weather can settle and a fruit is ripening for us.— Aleksei spoke with a voice so unlike his own that Nicholas turned immediately to the doctor who nodded.

—Yes, he's got a temperature, he's delirious. He needs medicines that are not here.— So much sense in those ravings, thought Nicholas. Maria, sitting at her brother's bedside, wiping his forehead, noticed a guard at the door into her parents' room. It was not Dimitri, but a face without expression, neither old nor young, a man never seen before. They were always different, those soldiers, it was difficult to learn their faces; they always seemed the same soldier, apart from Dimitri, that shy, hulking young fellow who would glance sideways at her with his big eyes. They had recently built a fence around the house to stop passersby looking in, and on the day it was put up, Maria noticed a certain embarrassment on the part of Dimitri during their walk; he kept on looking at her and then looking anxiously at the fence, then back at her. Strange people, these revolutionaries, Maria thought, they're not bad enough. . . . Now with the tall fence, only the sky was visible beyond the dismal garden. But the sky seemed to have undertaken to compensate the prisoners for their newly restricted view. From that day an incredible flock of birds seemed to make for the roof of Ipatiev's house, as if by a prearranged signal. It was not the migrating season, there was no reason why birds of completely different species, who had never been seen before in these parts, should come to nest precisely under the eaves of this prison. Even the guards kept on pointing out to each other the strange new inhabitants.

13

—⸺

Thousands of versts from Ipatiev's house, that evening Prince Ypsilanti too was thinking that this was not the migrating season, that it was strange so many varieties of birds were moving that day from Siberia toward Europe. And even though the survivors of the Preobrazhenskii Regiment were emotionally spent, and were no longer easily surprised, many soldiers noticed the phenomenon and drew each other's attention to the long lines in the sky.

—It's time we too migrate . . .— Ypsilanti remarked to his orderly who was polishing his boots. And while the corpulent colonel was being soothed by the sight of Alyosha's hands moving rapidly across the red leather, he thought back over the events of the last few hours. Another soldier had disappeared. But whereas the first one had vanished into the taiga after losing his senses, the second had gone mysteriously during the hunt for the tiger, a few minutes after talking, serenely and cheerfully as usual, to his companions. The prince was interrupted by a discreet cough. The aide-de-camp was ushering in Colonel Khabalov. Looking at him, the prince saw immediately that something very serious had happened, and for a second more he absented himself from the present, as if to postpone for as long as possible the moment of knowledge, the time of finding out what his deputy would tell him. But it was only a matter of seconds.

—I'm listening, my dear Khabalov.—

—Your Excellency, you must intervene as soon as possible. I have proof that some hundreds of men, perhaps as many as three or four companies, want to desert tonight and follow the Mongol Kaigiar into the taiga, taking their weapons, tents, food, equipment.—

—So few? I'm surprised. Are you sure you calculated right?—

Khabalov made no reply; he was thrown off balance by such a tone. Ypsilanti rose heavily from his chair, forcing Alyosha to one side. So, the moment had arrived. He was ready and already knew what to do. He knew full well he could still cause fear and he finally felt useful, as if that innate capacity for authority, worn so thin by the inertia into which his regiment had been plunged, could finally be brought into play, even if it was only to promote the semblance of a strategy that might give meaning to his last few days.

—It's a little early, they could have waited for me to decide. . . . Tell me, Khabalov, what proof do you have of this mutiny?—

—Two soldiers from my battalion kitchens have confessed. They've been seconded there the last few days, under orders from a sergeant major on your staff.—

—Efim! I never liked that ugly blind-man's mug. I did well to stop his promotion despite Karel's insistence. . . . Well, my dear Khabalov, if this is the situation, there's nothing for it but to have you relay to my four regimental battalion commanders the order to fall the men in on parade, in front of the flag, where I will address them.—

—What do you mean to do, Your Excellency?—

—How anxious you are to know ... don't worry, I've been getting ready for a while, ever since I told you of my decision to split the regiment, a decision you disapproved of so strongly....—

—As Your Excellency commands ...—

—Wait, I was about to forget the most important thing. Full uniform for the officers, the silver trumpet of Tsar Peter for saluting the flag and for saluting me, the band ... what remains of the band, to strike up the national anthem. Choreography is very important....— And after a pause the prince added: —You know, Khabalov, today will be a little like the Day of Judgment and I shall have the part of the Lord, separating the good from the bad. It is a demanding role. Go now, it's late.—

It was not easy to call a thousand men of a decimated and drifting regiment to muster, but the order had been peremptory, and within a few hours the four battalions were aligned in perfect array in front of the flag next to the four remaining members of the band, two trumpets, one drum, one fife. The silver trumpet that had been given to Count Preobrazhenskii, the first colonel of the regiment, by Peter the Great, sounded a salute to the flag as the soldiers stood to attention and presented arms. Further trumpet calls announced the arrival of the colonel on horseback. Ypsilanti told his deputy, Count Khabalov, to order "at ease," and began to talk, raising himself up a little on the saddle.

—Soldiers! We don't have much time to deceive ourselves!

I'm old and must die, as the laws of nature dictate, but you will by the laws of history, because traitors to the Emperor are to be crushed like this!— And Ypsilanti slashed the air with his whip, that hissed like a snake.

—It will be better for you to confess. I have here a list of those who were planning to desert. If they want me to spare their lives, those who were bent on leaving tonight must stand apart and form up over there— And he pointed to an area at the far end of the parade ground, next to the artillery. Heads swayed in deathly silence for an endless minute, during which Ypsilanti, sitting stock-still, feared for the first time that he might lose his self-control, that good and evil might no longer be identifiable. The officers around Ypsilanti were sweating profusely, as they turned their heads frantically, watching the troops, then the prince on horseback. Finally there was movement: in a confusion of faces, beards, belts, rifles, berets, shoes and tunics, hundreds of soldiers stepped out of their battalion formations to form smaller ranks at the far end of the parade ground.

Finally the traitors and those faithful to the Tsar were seen. The former were many, many more than Khabalov had calculated, more than half the regiment. In front of them, in the first rank, stood some officers, without their sabers which they had lain at the feet of the prince; they included Guderian, commander of the Second Battalion. So, they'll even have their commanders . . . Ypsilanti commented to himself.

The soldiers were silent now, as if something so great and simple had taken place there were no words, as if there was no longer room for entreaties, tears, farewells, insults. Those who had remained in the ranks of the faithful looked out at their companions with whom they had marched through Europe and Asia, with whom they had faced the fury of the Turks and the ice of Siberia. They had a bewildered look, as if from that moment even those who had stood firm and had not turned traitors inevitably had to start a new life, a different and more serious commitment, to confront a choice which could no longer be postponed. The others had been able to make a choice; whether traitors or not they had taken a grip on themselves, taken control of their own destiny, put an end to passivity, to that absurd holiday from life. And those who remained now had a choice thrust upon them.

Ypsilanti would accept no delay; he was thinking that even already among the troops remaining steadfast in their ranks, there must be a number of men of two minds. A few hours later, by nightfall, two days' provisions had been distributed and the former companies of his regiment had been allowed to disappear toward the darkness of the taiga, with no other witness than himself, Khabalov and two junior officers, while the remaining units were ordered to return to their quarters. Now Ypsilanti was serene, he felt he had done his duty, he had spared his poor soldiers without betraying the oath of loyalty to the Tsar.

—My dear Khabalov, now do you understand why this has been a little like the Last Judgment?—

—Yes, of course. But we, we shall never be able to choose,— the old second-in-command said while the steps of the rebellious companies could still be heard marching to freedom.

—Why not? Didn't you see what Guderian did?—

—I don't mean betray, Your Excellency . . .—

—Ah, no! My dear Khabalov, you don't want to run the risk, you want to be able to choose without enduring the other side's hate? Don't you know that history is full of traitors who became saints? The labels slip and what remains is truth. I'm telling you only because we're alone: I like Guderian much better now.—

—And you wanted me to go at their head?—

—Yes, if I could have chosen. But it was impossible and you, of course, had to come with me.—

—But where to, Your Excellency?—

—Where the same things are happening that happened here in the heart of Siberia, remote from civilization for more than two years.—

—Then you, too, believe what those Jews said, the unrest in Petrograd . . .—

—I believe my eyes, my dear Khabalov. And these eyes have seen so much in the last seventy years. Like yours, seeing we're about the same age. The whole of Russia was here today, in this mutiny against me and perhaps our Tsar. What happened here is probably happening at home, in Petrograd.—

While the two old men talked they could hear snatches of a song that was being sung by some of the soldiers on their way into the taiga. It was the song of the girl who waits in her village for her soldier to return. He returns after many years but she's no longer there; the soldier looks for her and when he can't find her he appeals to the Tsar to send out his cossacks to search for her. And the Tsar, so the song goes, strips himself of his clothes and exchanges them for those of the soldier, the better to look for her.

—Do you hear that? They sing, for tonight they're happy.

That's something, isn't it? You know, Khabalov, I must confess a curious fact: this evening, after my order to make separate formations, for a moment I was afraid they would not
move, that no one wanted to be a traitor. In that moment,
would you believe it, I had the greatest sense of terror I have
ever experienced.—

14

One day a great vibrant shadow trembled against the windows of the room occupied by the Tsar, the Tsaritsa and the Tsarevich. It was the agitation of the soldiers that drew their attention to it, especially the shouted orders of Jurovsky to shut themselves indoors. Aleksei had thrown the window open in his delirium and had seen a huge eagle on the roof of the greenhouse in the garden. Everyone had rushed in to draw Aleksei back, but they had remained stunned at the sight of the regal bird of prey with his wings outspread, about to take off. Nicholas did not move; he let the shadow of those wings climb to the roof, waited for Jurovsky to come and close the window. Some minutes of such intense silence passed that when Jurovsky arrived he could not speak, merely going to the window and slamming it shut noisily. The Romanovs remained motionless, looking at the window as if it were still open.

It's not so rare to see an eagle in the Urals, after all, Jurovsky thought going downstairs; nothing to get excited about. But those other birds? And only on this house of all the houses in town. They're becoming a nuisance with their evening concert. . . .

During the day the inhabitants of the second floor enjoyed the zest for life displayed by those winged fellow-prisoners; the medley of birdsong afforded them a new kind of company. They felt lighter, as if they themselves might take to the sky any minute. The birds had flown there; of all the houses in town they had chosen the one of the imprisoned Tsar; they had elected to share his imprisonment: it must be part of a plan, something was going to happen, Aleksei thought. Nicholas noticed the restlessness aroused in his wife and children by the presence of the birds. He sensed the way their cloistered life and their uncertainty about the future were tending to make them increasingly, day by day, look for some sign of divine intervention, and betrayed their helplessness and desperation. But then he would lose his own clarity of perception and be moved by the sight of his family looking at the birds, scanning the sky; and he himself would gaze up furtively, trying not to be seen, he too would be drawn into the atmosphere of expectation.

One night, though, the expectation turned to ecstasy. At the light of the moon a nightingale sang of the sweetness of the world, calling to Nicholas, Alice, Olga, Tatiana, Maria, Anastasia and Aleksei. Aleksei had never heard a nightingale and was enchanted, drawing near to the window.

—The eagle sent it. You can't see it, because it sings. The eagle can be seen and doesn't sing.— Nicholas listened to his son's strange logic and thought of the Imperial eagle and the unseen nightingale. He was right, he had never seen a nightingale or heard an eagle sing. If power came only from the eagle, then perhaps what was missing in the empire was the song of the nightingale. Power like that of the eagle and the nightingale combined could change the course of history; no one would be stronger than the Tsar who placed on his coat of arms the two winged animals. How much wisdom in those few lines on paper, in those animals drawn by hands who knew how to penetrate the forest of symbols and succeeded in convincing deer, eagle, lions, panthers, she-wolves, doves, gryphons to let themselves be captured for a moment. And then, forever, there they were on doorways of palaces, on the highest pinnacles of temples. Their glory pointed to the simple, domestic truth of their virtues: faithfulness, strength, courage, beauty, innocence, were raised up there for centuries, visible even to those who could not read. Because animals belonged to everyone, even those on coats of arms. The new power will have its coat of arms too, he thought, looking at the Red soldiers. Who knows what animal they will bear?

Everything was so provisional still in Russia, there had not been time to look for symbols. And so it was still his face that made the bank notes legal tender; the old ruble was still in circulation even though the Imperial motto had been stamped out in black. But there were no symbols or armorial bearings yet, only a length of script that could not embrace power in a couple of tokens. It's an art that only time can teach, it's understandable, Nicholas thought, and could not imagine a symbolic fauna for the new power. But he found it in Anastasia's drawings, for his daughter spent hours supplying illustrations to Aleksei's reading. The drawing showed an eagle among many other birds in flight toward the sun, over the taiga: below them, in a clearing, a long serpent was uncoiling as it fought a tiger. These will be on their coat of arms! The serpent and the tiger, earthly beasts, free of the delusion of flight, and strong as only a creation can be who partakes of our nature only, without nostalgia or distractions. . . . He, the Tsar, had been distracted so long as to have forgotten that everything could be forgiven a politician, but nothing would be forgiven an emperor: a Kerensky might succeed in escaping, but not they.

It was at the moment of abdication, when flight remained a possibility, that he had grown distracted, that he had wasted time: Mikhail had reproached him with it at Tsarskoe Selo before their departure for Tobolsk, when he had come to say good-bye.

—Nicholas, why did you hesitate? Why did you not flee when you abdicated, far from here?—

—And my family? How could I leave them behind?—

—You'd have been able to do much more for them as a free man.—

But this was not Nicholas's way of doing things, and both knew it. They embraced with tears in their eyes. Kerensky, then in power, was present at one end of the room where they were talking. Aleksei, who had a special liking for Uncle Misha, was spying through the keyhole in the antechamber. He would have wanted to run to his nice uncle, ask him what he had not been able to find out from anyone else: what did it mean that those soldiers, who used to be so devoted, had been laughing at him in the last few days and had prevented him from going into the park when he wanted to? What did it mean that so many courtiers had fled the palace as if they wanted to avoid them, and why did his mother and father ask permission for everything from that man who was in there with them? When he arrived, wearing his black cloak, walking with his quick stride, there was commotion in the palace. Who was he? They had told him his name, but how could he give orders if he was neither a general, nor a prince, nor one of his father's lieutenants? Suddenly Aleksei withdrew: his uncle had turned and was coming toward the door, after embracing his father.

—Are you here, Aleksei?— And hugging him, Mikhail whispered in his ear:

—Your father and mother need you, you must protect them, but unobtrusively. You are a man now, no longer a boy.—

In this way Mikhail had handed back the throne to his nephew, with a kiss on the ear and a hand through his hair. And Aleksei had dried his eyes without asking questions.

—I understand, Uncle Misha. Have a good journey and come back soon.— He tried to stand on his bad leg, forgetting the pain. Immediately after that the man in the black cloak had come out with his father, had shaken his hand and smiled at him for the first time.

When his mother came to take him out for his walk in the park, the soldiers on duty followed them in silence. Presently a crowd gathered on the other side of the gate, shouting insults at them. Aleksei turned to his guards, who had been stirred up and sneered, and glanced at his petrified parents. Then, slowly in order not to limp, he walked toward the crowd with his head high, looking straight ahead. He chose a face, a blond boy like himself, and concentrated his whole being on him. Why? Why? his fixed eyes asked. Come here, let's go to the pond and play, but stop this, aren't you ashamed? as he stood a few meters from the gate. Gradually the voices faded, everyone focused on Aleksei, on the pale face. A woman noticed the tension that emanated from him.

—Go, go back home, Tsarevich. Look at him, look how pale he is!—

There was a final murmur and a great silence fell: Aleksei collapsed, fainted from the effort to stand on a leg that could not support him. Alice rushed to him in sobs. She could no longer send a telegram to Rasputin; the friend had died who, from whatever corner of the empire, could send his blessing and heal Aleksei.

These days at Ekaterinburg, too, Aleksei's knee had swollen considerably and his temperature had gone up. But the boy, between delirium and lucidity, maintained a worrying capacity to predict things, as he had a little while before the extraordinary migration. The new turn the disease had taken reminded Nicholas too much of the gift of second sight that some blind men have; he preferred Aleksei talking to himself in the garden or asking him where the real Falklands were. He did not know that Aleksei was still talking, but to the birds now. They seemed to know that he had been waiting for them there, and began immediately telling him of their endless journey, the vast Siberian plain they had crossed, the village with the telegraph they had not been able to reach, the horrible winter they had passed, waiting for spring to return, of a commander no one could disobey. They seemed friends meeting again after a short separation, scattered, swarms from one great flock that was heading there to the house where the Tsar was.

The terrible time was at night, when all the birds were silent in their nests and Aleksei felt as if he lived in two houses, a day house and a night house. Who knows what countries the birds dreamt of at night? How long was the vigil, waiting for sleep, with nothing to look at, the bed as vast as the world. He did not know which part to lie in, and the hours called to him not to leave the birds alone. When Mother rose to keep him company, he was annoyed. When she was there, the birds seemed ashamed and kept silent. She could ruin everything any minute, as she had done lifting the curtain behind which he was playing with Joy. —Don't touch the animals, Aleksei, you can catch something.— His mother seemed capable of making him feel the full weight of whatever he was doing, playing, dressing, getting up. Only when he was ill did she become more patient, but it was an effort, it was not spontaneous. Then he felt sorry for her and let her believe he was enjoying her company.

15

Kaigiar's first gesture when the rebel soldiers reached the taiga was to throw away the hundred pieces of silver with the bearded image of the crowned Tsar of all the Russias, Nicholas II. He had had to accept the reward from the colonel but he had not touched it. "Amba," the tiger, was not his, now that it was dead: it belonged to the gods of the forest, woe betide him if he kept the money. The metal coins fell all around and the three Georgian soldiers were on the point of picking them up when a voice shouted derisively:

—What on earth are you going to do with those pieces of metal in here?—

It was true, they were now useless. Nonetheless, the three soldiers shared them out, quarreling.

They were looking for other things in the taiga, those soldiers, now that they knew they could live there like Ignatic who had followed a woman. . . . Kaigiar had told them, though not at first, when Ypsilanti questioned them each in turn about Ignatic, first the captain, then Misha, then the Yakut hunters, then the rest of the soldiers and finally Kaigiar. But Kaigiar had retreated to being the speechless idiot he had always been in front of officers, the obedient soldier engaged in the most menial chores in the kitchen, to whom nothing could be taught to raise him above his primitive level. Nothing comprehensible came out of his mouth. It was only afterward, a day or two later, in the mess, while he crouched near his three tent companions, that he said thoughtfully, in his execrable Russian:

—Ignatic was taken by a woman.—

The others paid no attention at the time. But when he explained how he had seen the young Kirgiz girl when he had gone in search of stones and herbs needed to skin "amba," because nothing that hid in the taiga like an animal could escape him, the three began to take notice. The information had seemed of little importance to Kaigiar, who had only told them to demonstrate his knowledge of the forest, his expertise as a hunter from whom nothing in the forest could escape. Whether or not there were human beings there did not seem to him all that important. He had already told them about the woman, and, somewhat irritated by all the excitement, he turned his full attention to eating his meat and drinking his kvass.

—But listen, Kaigiar, don't you like women?— Juri asked, grinning, with a wink at his companions. Kaigiar did not even look at him as he carried on searching in his mess tin with his knife, picking up bits of meat. Only later as they walked to their tent did he tell Juri that both his women had died in childbirth, back in his village near the great lake, and how he looked for them in the elks of the forest, because women who die in childbirth live on in the female elks; that's where he looked for his two wives, Jela and Masha. After those words Juri and the others saw yet another facet of this indefinable, timeless creature, and they no longer felt like asking him the question all three had on the tips of their tongues, how old could he possibly be. Kaigiar, however, anticipated them, as if he could read their minds:

—I've seen seventy springs and seventy winters.— But before that, he told them, Kaigiar was a wolf, and before that he was a woman, and before that he was a fish . . . and his eyes narrowed to become slits so small he looked like a blind man who has freed himself from the deceit of light.

What he said about Ignatic took no time at all to spread through that battalion and then to the others, casting its seed in most units of the regiment. And as if the young men needed nothing more than the story of Private Ignatic and the young Kirgiz girl to break the spell of the regiment lost in the middle of nowhere, within a few days the decision to leave had been taken, as well as the decision on the breakdown of units, the allocation of duties and responsibilities, the sentry roster, the departure time. Had it not been for the soldiers on kitchen detail who had betrayed more from fear of Kaigiar than of Ypsilanti, everything would have gone as the mutineers had planned it. Kaigiar had become their strange leader, even though he had no duties. But it was from him that those few hundred soldiers derived their strength to flee, from his way of addressing himself to things and animals, of relating distant events in his own life as if they belonged to someone else, of recalling facts and circumstances from his long life as if they had occurred outside of history, outside of states, boundaries, flags, tsars; they detected in the little insignificant Mongol a power equal to that of the aristocratic Ypsilanti. And certainly he must be roughly the same age, "seventy springs," as the old St. Petersburg prince born of a Greek marchioness and raised in Paris during the last years of Napoleon III's reign.

There must be a reason, a meaning to the little Asian hunter's being intercepted by the history of Imperial Russia and the world war, to be enrolled into the most glorious regiment of the Tsar—it could not have been by mere chance. It was as if his life had to end with a different transmigration, as if his duty was to help a group of men still living to transfer their souls from one body to another.

—Kaigiar is really extraordinary,— Lieutenant Ivan Deniskin said to his colleague, the doctor, the night before the revolt, —he's managed to convince us all. . . .—

—Some may get cold feet,— his friend answered. And that was exactly what happened that night: two infantrymen slipped between tents to present themselves to Khabalov and reveal the whole plot.

The first few days in the taiga the hunters trained by Kaigiar managed to track down enough game to last them several weeks. The Mongol was concerned not only with food but also with making a start on preparing for winter right now in July: he knew only too well the ruthlessness, the rigor, of winter in the forest, the lethargy of hibernating animals, the gnawing of the icy waters of the river, the sleep of the trees, the absolute suspension of life. He did not therefore share in the foolish restlessness of the young men who lived in the constant hope of coming across the village where the women's huts were at some distance from the men's, as Kaigiar had told them. Symptoms of the small hunter's impatience manifested themselves within a few days. He worked to erect huts similar to the isbas, that would protect them from the worst of the cold and allow them to spend the winter there, but virtually all the soldiers chose not to help, postponing the work, content to hunt and spread out freely in the forest looking for prey farther and farther afield, in the secret hope of a meeting like the one that had happened to Ignatic, to which no one else would be witness. So preparation for winter moved slowly, and Kaigiar felt bitterly that a danger greater than the tiger was stalking these young men who did not listen to him. It was as if the thought of a woman had completely blinded them, as if the "amba" was revenging her death, after calling them into the taiga, confusing them, setting their blood alight with desires through which they would lose themselves. And so some of them began to stray, not to return. Colonel Guderian, who maintained some shadow of authority over them and made a roll call every evening, began to register the first absentees. Perhaps they had already found their woman in there, the others thought with envy, not believing that they could have fallen prey to some bear or wolf or to some fierce and mistrustful savage, even though Kaigiar had warned them of the possibility more than once.

Rather, they imagined that in the forest their absent comrades had realized their dream of a love that carried them even farther from the real world, wherein the last remaining witnesses to the war and their duty—their companions whose presence reflected as in a mirror their condition of condemned fugitives—had finally been eliminated. So, instead of serving as a warning, the constant disappearances excited them to look immediately for the realization of that dream, before the winter, before the horror of the Siberian frost, could return and trap them a third time.

Kaigiar had given up trying to save them by now, after his last warnings, to which some of the soldiers had reacted quite violently. Kaigiar recovered his peace of mind and continued his preparations for the winter almost alone, without interfering further in the life of those men who seemed to want to take flight one by one, called by a mysterious destiny like the one that called the birds to the Urals, the same birds they had observed a little while before when they were still with Ypsilanti. Kaigiar had made up his mind, before he should end up alone thinking of the uselessness of his efforts and wisdom; something or someone was calling him too, toward new forms of suffering and madness, where others yet would have need to understand their own fate at the hands of men or beasts, a fate more ancient than their own era, prisoners as they were of God, each in a separate cell. Among the soldiers there was one who had succeeded in finding Ignatic and his Kirgiz woman but had not been able to come back and tell his companions. It was Misha, Ignatic's closest companion.

When Ypsilanti had forced them to choose either to remain or go into the taiga, Misha had been one of the first to line up with the rebels, and they had laughed long and hard at his imitation of the colonel:

—Soooldiers! A law of nature condemns me while yoooouuu, yooouuu've been buggered by a laaaw of history. . . .— And on the way into the taiga he had been one of the first to strike up the song of the Tsar and the soldier; he did not want Ypsilanti and those lackeys of his to think they were afraid. But in the forest Misha had suddenly changed, had been unable to participate in the general euphoria. On the very first day he had found Ignatic's beret swaying on a bush not far from the river, for all the world as if it had been stuck there playfully by its own wearer. From that moment Misha had known no peace. Two days later, he had ventured deeper and deeper, farther along the river in his search, learning to leap from branch to branch like Kaigiar, and a shiny object, dangling from a branch like a snake, had caught his eye: it was Ignatic's belt. And then he was the first one to go out in the morning and the last to return at night. Some noticed how strange it was that he never brought back any game like the others, but returned scratched in the face, with his clothes torn, his shirt soaked in sweat, as if he had not spared himself in some hunt. Once Kaigiar had looked at him long and hard while Misha sharpened an arrow. He had noticed the restlessness, the inability to let go and join in the joking and the slapstick of his companions around the fire in the evening while they ate, listening to one of them singing. And he had seen death over the head of the boy.

Now Misha hid if he sensed the presence of any soldier, until he was sure the intruder had moved away. He absolutely had to find Ignatic at whatever cost, he absolutely had to see him alive again; he felt as if he was close and that the wall separating them was so thin a breath of wind would have blown it down. How much time seemed to have passed since they had fired upon the enemy side by side, since they had marched side by side through snow, to Vachitino, since they had waited for Ypsilanti's decision in front of the taiga. . . . How he missed the innocent laugh, that begging to be left alone, not to tell his companions how he had spent the whole night writing to his family, how he had blushed bright red in Vachitino when a Gypsy had read his hand and told him, with a stealthy caress to his face, that soon he would be greatly loved. . . .

As he searched for him, lost in the memories of three years of communal life, he did not realize how dangerously far he was venturing, too far from the camp, nor how diminished the numbers were when he returned to the fire and to Guderian's roll call. One morning he stopped in his wanderings to rest and eat. It was very hot: it seemed as if the general weariness of merely existing under the burning heat brought the fierce and the gentle beasts to a truce, as if in such a moment even the fight for survival were suspended. Suddenly Misha thought he heard among the sounds of the forest the unmistakable tones of a man's voice, of men's voices speaking an unknown tongue. He immediately picked up his bow and arrows, hid the food and climbed the tallest tree nearby. In a few minutes he reached the top and looked around at a sea of blue and green, transfixed, like Ignatic, by the desire not to climb down, never to touch the ground again. Below, in an opening among the trees, there were some huts in a line. There were women bowed to the earth, engaged in arranging the seeds of some fruit to dry in the sun. He could see their hair, their arms, their backs. At the other end of the village Misha saw men building a fence, hammering posts into the ground. Misha leaned out as far as he could; he had seen a figure emerging from behind one of the huts. The figure slowly turned and lifted his eyes in a confident and assured look to the tree where Misha was perched, while a woman drew near to him. It was Ignatic. And the very second Misha felt those eyes catch his, he felt a crack as a branch snapped, and his body dropped in a vertigo of colors and sounds until it smashed into the ground. His body, which he had inhabited for twenty-two years, lay there, at the foot of the tree—but Misha was already far away.

That very evening Kaigiar threw into the air a colored stone on which were marked the four points of the earth. The stone fell on blue, south, and that would be the direction of his journey. The next morning the few remaining soldiers looked for him, because he had disappeared. But in their heart of hearts they were not sorry, as if they could be freer now to take flight toward their future.

16

—•—

Nicholas tried to remain alone as little as possible. Not that it was difficult in those five rooms, but whereas before he had often been irked by it, now the presence of others took his mind off a deep anguish. Any moment an image visible only to him could appear reflected in the mirror. Even the advent of the eagle was nothing more than preamble, a forewarning of the advent of something else. And he was tired, he had not more strength to reject that sinister power which he had clear-sightedly condemned as Tsar in the fullness of his sovereignty. Sometimes it was as if the nightmare would soon come to an end; a few more minutes and the Whites would dash in and wake him from the anguish: God had sent him through the door of false dreams to put the faith of his vicar on earth to the test. Each time, in front of the mirror, he would quickly lower his eyes, but never fast enough to avoid noticing the presence drawing near from a great distance. And he would see again the illusory suite of rooms at Tsarskoe Selo from the one in which he had sat each morning as the court barber trimmed his beard. There had been two large mirrors face-to-face so that as he looked at himself, sitting there, he could see reflection upon reflection of the room itself. The power of the Evil One seemed to him like this, multiplying itself endlessly, yet not real.

—It's not wise to stay here: tomorrow morning early we'll leave.— Who had spoken? Nicholas looked around to see if the others had heard, but Demidova continued to put away crockery, the attendant to wipe crumbs from the table; Alice was reading her prayer book. Yet he had heard the voice, he had not dreamt it.

That day he asked the doctor to support his request to Jurovsky for permission to go into the garden and chop wood; the physical exercise would surely distract him.

—So, Nicholas Romanov wants to do some work? Certainly, we'll give him a saw and some wood.—

And he sawed for hours in the garden, trying not to think of the mirror, to forget Rasputin's voice.

Tatiana, the more reserved of the daughters, noticed her father's restlessness before the others, noticed his need never to be alone, always to be doing something. She, on the other hand, knew how to be silent and listen, knew how to sit in the same position for hours, thinking. She had loved Rasputin more than her mother had, and she had never forgiven her father for not condemning to death the two assassins, Dimitri and Felix. She despised her father's silence more than her mother did; she was not ready, like her stupid sisters, to die there, in Ekaterinburg. She knew from where help could still come; Rasputin had taught her the power to change things, though it had been easier when he was alive to read the formula, speak the necessary words. Now he was no longer there and she had to be brave if she ever wanted to save herself and her family. She had already tried to speak with him and he had answered from where there were neither the living nor the dead. One day even her father had heard the voice, and from then on he had begun sawing wood, poor thing, to get it out of his head. She felt sorry for her father, for the Tsar, reduced to asking permission to open a window. But she would erase the shame.

One night in St. Petersburg, three years before, Rasputin had appeared in her room:

—I've known for a long time, my little Tatiana, that you love me, you've come to me on many nights in dreams, to tell me, and I don't know how many times I've woken with the intention of coming to you, and I never had the courage.—

—Since that lunch with my parents, when Uncle Aleksei died, since that time when, after lunch, we were left alone for a minute . . .—

—Yes, since that day I dream of you every night and I can't close my eyes without hearing your voice. At home the mirrors know it and they sing and smile when you sing and smile here, alone in your room; my little child, I have you always in front of my eyes, I know what you do, what you wear . . .—

So Tatiana learned in Rasputin's last year of life how one can whip the air and the spirit with words, reading the books of the cabala, until she had acquired the intonations needed to make the rivers run dry and to drive the mountains into the sea. She loved him for his terrible, fearless strength that accepted no boundaries, not even the boundary of death which he had predicted and to which he was indifferent except for his desire to be near her more often. He knew how to move through the maze of nine hundred rooms to hers, without being seen. And she did not care anymore for her father, her mother, her position: it was he who held back from a thousand plans of elopement. Tatiana was nineteen, but her will, lit by the fascination of that superhuman man, made her capable of any madness. He, in the daughter of the Tsar, loved the power that had kept his race chained for centuries, the strength that ran through the fields and the harbors of Russia like a wind. And he would immerse himself in her as in an abyss that not even his powers could fill. She was never to know how long Rasputin had lived with the terror of losing her. A few days before being murdered, he talked to her in a way she had never forgotten:

—You will be in great danger if I die; only my help, if you have learned well all that I have taught you, only my help will save you. You will be the strong one next to a weakened Tsar.— And she, holding back her tears, had asked him to stay close to her.

—Your father's days as ruler are numbered; you've understood, his power is not absolute. But I am here, Tatiana, I am near you. And I will be with you when you need me and call me.—

When they had come to tell the sisters that Rasputin had been killed, she, who had known it from the night before, had smiled, looking at her mother in a faint, and thought of her father's crown, the double-headed eagles in papier mâché that did not have the strength to save the only real man in the empire. She felt as if Rasputin had grown tired of this minuscule world and left for another, where he could open his arms wider. Afterward, during the imprisonment, Tatiana had used the powers he had taught her every once in a while, just to go on talking to him, not to do anything useful. Now, for the first time, she thought she should use them in Ekaterinburg;

she should do something to break the ring that was tightening around Ipatiev's house. The moment had come, but in a last gesture of respect for her father's authority, she would have liked him to be convinced of it, to realize there was nothing else to be done. The things that had happened in that house, however, had alarmed her; it was as if someone else was getting ready to bring her down and deploying other forces she would have been unable to recognize. Those birds on the roof, and the eagle, and then, at night, the nightingale's song and Aleksei's strange ravings—too many forces of which she was ignorant had concentrated themselves on Ipatiev's house. And of course she was aware of her father's restlessness.

Oh, if only they knew that she wanted to save them; if she could explain to her dear ones that her wiliness, Rasputin's wiliness, could still save them. But she could not speak, not only not to alarm them, but also because of the resistance she felt in her father, through that quiet and heroic chopping of wood, and in Aleksei through the serenity with which he endured the full crisis of his illness.

And so Tatiana waited for the right moment to act.

17

—

Ypsilanti had given orders for the departure for Tobolsk
on the next day, and the soldiers were mounting the guns
on their carriages, dismantling the great armory tents, the
headquarters tents, the infirmary, the kitchens. They were
storing the game, salting the potatoes, lifting onto carts the
large barrels of water from the river, cleaning their weapons,
listening to their officers' final orders. Some were trying to
delouse themselves, and everywhere there was the acrid smell
of leather and grease, of horses' dung. Almost every tent had
only one man left where there had been three the previous
days. Those who had not abandoned the regiment turned with
their thoughts to their companions, for whom there would
never be a homecoming, for whom, if they were captured,
there would be a lifetime sentence in a Siberian fortress, in
forced labor camps. For them there could only be the life of
savages and deserters, if they survived the rigors of winter and
of the taiga. For themselves at least there was the hope of
seeing, once again, wife, mother, children; they could hope to
return home in peace: the war would end one day. That
damned Kaigiar had ruined their comrades; Ypsilanti should

have had the Mongol shot for leading them into the forest to begin with. Instead even the prince had fallen for him, to the point of offering him a hundred silver rubles to kill the tiger. The surviving soldiers, mostly older than the rebels, were those who had heard little or nothing about Ignatic, whom the Mongol's revelations had not reached. They had just this image of Kaigiar, the wild and dreamlike image of the organizer of the hunting expedition, of this man who could barely speak Russian, who directed the soldiers in the hunt through gestures and animal grunts. They were tired of these Asian peculiarities, they could no longer stand such a hostile, unfamiliar world, they dreamt of returning to their isbas, to sleep above the stove, to lay in peat during the summer and cook and chat around the fire in winter, waiting for spring. The fields were waiting for them, so thick with wheat every summer that it was difficult to see how one pair of arms could reap all that gold from the earth blessed by God. And if they had their masters, the counts, the princes, the grand dukes, those lords like Ypsilanti and Khabalov who came sometimes to see the harvest, offering vodka to the starets and the peasants, and then taking most of this bounty, it was also true that they left enough to pay the taxes to the Tsar and not die of hunger for a year. Ah, to be able to return to the wife with the money from the sale of wheat and say to her:

—There, put this money away now, now we can stop worrying for another year. . . .—

—If war doesn't come, little one, if you don't have to go away as your father did thirty years ago, as your brother did,— the women would reply. This was the only threat to a hard but peaceful life: war. War had snatched them from their homes, leading them to shoot and kill unknown men in a world that was too big. But now Ypsilanti had given the order for departure; this time they would really return home, they told themselves as they polished the buckles of their belts, as they cleaned their boots, oiled the breech of their rifles. And maybe it was better that only the few who were really loyal to the Tsar remained, those who had no strange ideas in their heads, who could not wait to see their villages as they had always been. It seemed easier to find their own world again if those who seemed able to envisage a different one drew aside. The more they thought about it, the more they thought that they were right in wanting to return, and the others were wrong, those comrades whose faults they now remembered more clearly. And so they concluded that they, those others, had always been hotheads for whom an order had rarely been right, for whom a sacrifice had rarely been necessary or a task useful.

Tobolsk was so near in everyone's mind that they were not going to have time to consume even a small part of those provisions; they were even going to be able to offer them as gifts to the town people, to those who would be kind and welcome them to their homes, who would listen to all the tales they had to tell. They had so many, so many more than any other regiment of the Tsar: they were the Preobrazhenskii; they hadn't rebelled against Ypsilanti, they hadn't broken their oath. And they imagined themselves a little as heroes, looked on with admiration by girls, welcomed with full honors. There would certainly be an Imperial governor at Tobolsk who had heard through the Vachitino telegraph that they were marching to reach the Tsar. The Tsar: they almost did not dare hope that he would still be there after so many months. It would be too much like a dream come true, to meet him, to come into his presence and show him the extent of their love. They had searched for him for two years, and when one part of the regiment had grown tired of that search, they had continued. The Little Father at Tobolsk . . . ah, to find him there! So much time had passed since they had found out through the telegraph that he was there and needed them, needed loyal troops. What could have happened at St. Petersburg? A revolt, it seemed, one of the many revolts that the Tsar had always been able to quash.

The officers too were getting ready to reenter Tobolsk, but their spirits were much more troubled. The dozen men had never forgotten what Ypsilanti had said in the office of the governor of Vachitino, the truth they had sworn not to reveal to the soldiers. That last night as they walked back to their tents to sleep, they could hear the noises of the beasts in the taiga, those animals they had seen and caught on their hunting expeditions but which at night seemed again mysterious and unreachable. What would happen if a new tiger should appear tonight, now that Kaigiar had gone? What were their fellow officers doing in there? Tomorrow they would leave and never again hear the taiga throb at night, they would lose their last contact with their companions.

Ypsilanti too was hearing those noises and thinking that it was the last night, but he had no wish to hear those sounds again, nor did he ever want to hear news of the troops that had fled into the forest. He was absolutely calm. And unlike many other nights of that month of July, he fell asleep very early, and dreamt he was in Crimea, at Livadia, with the Imperial family, the Tsar, the Tsaritsa, the Tsarevich, the Grand Duchesses Olga, Tatiana, Maria and Anastasia. But he was no longer Prince Ypsilanti, he was an old English archaeologist who was digging in the sand with his team, bringing to light a small Roman town. The Imperial family had come to visit the site and while they were there a statue was unearthed, a statue without forearms, supine, not yet aroused from its underground sleep, still not completely uncovered.

—It's been here two thousand years,— he was explaining to the Tsar, who had wanted to stay and look while the archaeologists uncovered, inch by inch, the knees, the folds of the peplum, the feet.

—It's an emperor, Your Majesty, a Roman emperor; it looks like Trajan,— he explained, and Nicholas II murmured:

—He too . . .—

—But it's curious,— Ypsilanti added, as the marble emperor was being carefully cleaned of all the earth, —it's curious, Your Majesty can see, here, the left knee protrudes beyond the peplum, in an unusual way, and the right shoulder is lower . . .—

—Is he lame, then?—

—The Emperor Claudius was lame, mon père. . .— Olga said shyly.

—It's true, Your Imperial Majesty. It's him, Claudius . . . not an important emperor, a rather nondescript figure, so gentle, so unfit for governing, it's indeed strange that there should be such a beautiful marble statue of him three meters high, here in the provinces . . . but no, there's no mistaking it, it is Claudius, who was lame, like the statue . . .— Ypsilanti said. And in the dream he felt Nicholas gaze for a long time on that statue of a gentle ruler so unfit to govern an empire as vast as the known world, noticing the protruding leg and shoulder, that physical inadequacy so ill-suited to power and yet that had been vested with it.

—The head, though, is very beautiful, it has a certain majesty and pride,— the Tsar observed thoughtfully.

—This is not very important, Your Imperial Majesty, because it was tradition among the Romans to substitute the head of the emperor with the head of the next emperor. It could very well be Trajan's head . . .— Ypsilanti explained, and he heard Nicholas II add smiling:

—Who in turn took on himself the beauty that did not belong to him and will forever have to be beautiful . . . ah, no one will know who we were. . . .—

At that point the dream lapsed into confusion, the figures of the Tsar, the Tsaritsa, the Grand Duchesses Olga, Tatiana, Maria and Anastasia dwindled away until they disappeared, and Ypsilanti reverted in his dream to being colonel and regimental commander, and seemed to embark on an endless journey.

18

Alice found it difficult to stand up, these hot July days since her collapse. At the time of the daily walk the soldiers now took her in a chair to the door of the garden; she had always hated that melancholy parade and now her weakness gave her an excuse to avoid it. There was one place to which she would have liked to return during those moments, to see if Katerina, her nurse, was still alive. The Hesse family had an estate near Darmstadt where Alice had been brought up by Katerina, the village medicine woman, who was familiar with every herb, and effected cures, resting content to see her patients go away happy. Katerina had been widowed as a very young woman and her son Henry had died at seven months of typhoid fever, soon after his father. Alice was born just then and Katerina had been chosen to breast-feed her. The mother, a daughter of Queen Victoria, had been in great danger throughout labor and had refused to see the newly born baby for a while. As the years passed, Katerina grew to love her charge with the love that Henry had awoken in her for a few instants, and this love grew ever greater when the child lost her mother at six. Katerina and Alice often went into the woods near the ducal estate, where the nurse spent long periods; together they looked for the herbs most suited to the sicknesses in the village near the castle, but they also found herbs more rare, more powerful, to heal sicknesses that the peasants had not yet experienced, but which might befall them someday. From the nurse she had learned what a fine point there was between poison and medicine in a flower, learned that the tenderest, sweetest corolla could hide a force so brutal it could kill before the cut flower withered, and that the most modest and fragile of flowers could reawaken in a dying body the most joyous wish to live.

The child had quickly understood that the external appearance is no help in judging the strength which is invisible. Katerina was the only one who could protect her everywhere from a curious feeling of threat and hostility that she had felt since birth.

As she grew, Alice had had to go away from the Darmstadt estate on more and more frequent journeys with her family. When she came back Katerina did not ask where she had been, what marvels she had seen in the places she had visited, but would immediately show her the new herbs of the season in a basket, as if they had parted only the day before. Alice owed to Katerina her deep love of the earth, the profound sense of it as mother, as grave; she knew that life and death are carried in that womb and she admired the variety of flowers and plants that could cohabit a little patch of ground without any danger of their juices becoming blended and losing power: a few centimeters away from a poisonous herb, there was a flower whose corolla made the blood run strongly through the veins. Death and life were there, in the same field, looking at each other.

She would have liked to have vision powerful enough to be able to trace underground the close but separate channels through which the poisonous and the benign juices flowed. So many times Katerina had told her to seek not only the herbs for the ills in the village—podagra, pneumonia, colds, irregular fluxes, rheumatism—because the world was big and herbs grow everywhere, like sicknesses. She did not know, but was certain that among those she kept and dried, there were some precious ones, and she was sorry they were going to remain unused while perhaps there was some suffering person whom those very herbs could have healed in an instant.

So when Alice, the future Tsaritsa Alexandra, had left Hesse for Russia twenty-four years ago, she had brought with her, amid her thousand pieces of luggage, a large basket of every kind of herb, labeled in Katerina's strong clear script, with the name and the dosage correct for every contingency. She had set aside from the rest, in a yellow sachet, three or four herbs not yet well tested: these possessed extraordinary powers, vouched for in writing by Katerina. Her advice was, however, only to use these terrible herbs as a last resort, in face of unconquerable ills.

—Remember there are ills of which we know nothing. The earth knows them, and perhaps has given us remedies.—

That little sachet, now more black than yellow, had always made her hands tremble a little, at Tsarskoe Selo, at Tobolsk and now here, on this July afternoon, sitting in the doorway to the garden of Ipatiev's house. She thought back to her Katerina who, if she had been present (the last news of her was a few years old), could have advised her. She thought of Aleksei's illness, of Rasputin who was no longer there, of Nicholas, more and more absentminded, methodically chopping wood in front of her. What could she do for Aleksei? Not even the medicines could give him back the use of his legs, the boy was suffering too much. Was it the moment to use one of Katerina's herbs? In Nicholas's calm despair, in the ravings of Aleksei with his capacity to predict everything, in their expectation of faithful followers who would come when it was too late, Alice was beginning to understand which were the unrecognized illnesses. So, perhaps each one of her dear family would have to take Katerina's herbs; she should make infusions for them all. . . . Alice trembled, tightening her grip on the sachet and looked at her daughters one by one, then lifted her eyes to Aleksei's room. Every once in a while the sounds of the Whites' artillery reached her, like a cruel joke that reverberated in the eyes of the soldiers. She thought then that she could sacrifice herself for her children, that she could drink those herbs: they were, after all, given her by the person who had loved her and welcomed her when her mother had not wanted her at the breast. What harm could they do? But she knew what remedy she sought from Katerina, the only one her nurse would give her if she loved her still. And perhaps she had put it in the sachet before the Tsaritsa left to reign over Russia, the accursed land where good can only be absolute, like evil, because both were bestowed by kings. Only kings can choose death as a last remedy if there is no other way: that was why they used to wear the poisoned ring on their finger.

—Your Imperial Majesty, the Tsarevich sends me to beg you to come up to his room,— Demidova said, and the sachet fell from Alice's startled hands. The maid immediately bent over to hand it back to her but Alice snatched it from her fingers and the violence of her gesture tore the ancient fabric.

Everything that was inside spilled out: a little dust that not even the slender fingers of the Tsaritsa could gather. Alice could not believe her eyes: nothing, there was nothing left in Katerina's precious bag, the terrible power of those herbs had spent itself through the twenty-three years of her reign. The maid could not reconcile herself to having split the little bag that was so precious to her mistress, but at the same time she failed to understand what was so valuable about its contents. It must have been a memento of some person dear to her, the relic of a saint. There was only dust, I don't understand ... Slowly Demidova went back upstairs, following the chair on which two soldiers were bearing the Tsaritsa.

Aleksei was waiting for her, lying in bed, looking at the doctor as if to say, Please, can you leave us alone? and the doctor left.

—Mother, you must not be afraid. Why do you want to leave me?—

At these words Alice closed her eyes, trying to get a grip on herself: her son really frightened her.

—Aleksei, why do you speak to me like this?—

—Because you thought of leaving before us, Mother. . . .—

A deep silence fell: a trapped bird flapped against the window. Aleksei watched that whir of wings as if his thoughts were very far away and he had no more to say to his mother. Alice called Demidova and the doctor and left her son with them. He had put her to greater shame than ever in her life. He had looked at her as a mother should never be looked upon. She was really frightened. She would have to talk about it with Nicholas if she did not want to go mad: her son had reproached her with wanting to kill herself, and read her thoughts, it was terrible.

Later Nicholas learned that the Tsaritsa was in a highly emotional state. Trup came to tell him during a break in the cutting of the wood. The attendant came upon the Tsar as he stood leaning against the stumps, his gaze lost in an indefinable point of the garden; and he had stood at a respectful distance, waiting. Nicholas was listening to the water of the Iset that ran past Ekaterinburg at a little distance from Ipatiev's house. He had only seen the river when they had come into the city from Tobolsk, but had learned to listen to it day by day, especially since the fence had been built. It seemed to sing louder and louder, the river, and it distracted him from what he was engaged in; he could no longer count the number of times he had stopped that afternoon, leaned against the stumps and the handle of the saw. The river ran as he had run to this point, self-assured and yet imprisoned within the banks, exempted from choice and faithful to his calling—that of a great but confined force. The infinite freedom of the waters of the sea, that could welcome the richness of the river of monarchy, would never know the pleasure of being limited by two banks, the happiness in the sacrifice to which so many small watercourses submitted, prisoners of the earth. That channeling, that consenting to many, those curves, those loops and the progressive slowing down of the current, the refusal to hurry, all this had been full of the love of life. The Tsar and the river had never refused to satisfy the anxiety of the earth, they had listened to everyone.

He remembered the day of the coronation, when for three days he and Alice had walked through crowds of people come to greet them. He had understood the strength of boundaries only with the passing of the years, when he had realized, the day of the coronation, that he was no longer Nicholas, but a power confined by banks. When he had understood that he was no one, that he no longer had a right to any personality, like the river that keeps flowing but knows not where, called by the sea and held by the earth, he had felt bereft. No man on earth could undertake to annihilate himself to that extent. To be free and strong like the sea was right, not weak like the river. But during his reign he had understood further that no freedom was stronger than the freedom of a king. What use was power if it could not be determined through renunciation? If one is not lured back to a kingdom with limits, if one's country does not prompt an urge to return to it, what desire remains, to wander freely in the world? Nicholas knew that only by alluding to freedom could freedom be loved: it was impossible to look forever on the vast expanse of the sea. His people who for years had lived a life justly circumscribed had now wanted to break out, to extend their gaze to the open sea, and he had dried up. No one was willing anymore to see their dream realized by proxy; impatience had broken the banks and the attenuated thrust of power now lay listlessly like a shallow lake on so much of the land. But these surface waters lay so shallow that no one could delude himself into believing the vast plains flooded by the river of the empire had the depth of a sea. Nicholas was sure no ship would sail on those mirrors. The revolution would one day recall the water to its bed, and the river would begin to run to the sea again. He, who embodied power, knew what chains are attached to freedom, just as he knew how much violence contributed to a perfect act of justice: there was no gesture of power that did not trample on someone, and freedom itself was tied to that strange law that demands the finite to represent the infinite. At that moment Nicholas heard a child cry in a nearby house. That child would never be able to explain to its mother why it was crying. And the mother will never know why her child weeps, but they will continue to cry and to ask why, Nicholas thought. The crying led him back to Trup, who was waiting.

—What is it, Trup?— Nicholas could see the guards approaching, his time outside was at an end. As he climbed the stairs he could still hear the river sing. In the kitchen he turned on the tap to drink a glass of water. He let it run to drink it cooler, ever cooler, and could not make up his mind, as he thought of the coolness of the water if he were to give it a little longer to run. He stood there with the empty glass in his hand. He felt as if he were helping the river he could not see. Alice had dozed off, and the mortified Demidova was telling the Tsar that it had been her fault, she had carelessly caused to be torn that little sachet that the Tsaritsa so treasured. Nicholas did not want to waken his wife and began to read, but he could not follow what he was reading; he felt the cold presence of the mirror behind him: someone was drawing near from an infinite distance. The light suddenly dimmed, and a somber grayness—storm light—invaded the room. What a sudden change!

The birds are silent, as they are before a storm. Suddenly there is the first cloudburst, so violent as to make one believe the Iset has changed its course and is flooding the house. Alice wakes with a cry for help at the sound of shutters banging, doors slamming in a sudden draft. Aleksei looks at his mother from the bed, in silence; Tatiana stares at the reflection in the mirror of her father who turns to catch her looking at him: all in a flash.

It is almost impossible to see in the gloom, and yet on the horizon, beyond the windows, there is the July light, that insolent light that he is sure he has never found so intrusive, not in any month of his life. It is as if the storm is focused on Ipatiev's house and only a few meters beyond, the sky is clear and calm. Only Tatiana is serene, as if nothing has happened; she reads and rereads a letter from her friend Anna Tatischeva which she received when they were still in Tobolsk. Nicholas cannot tell how much time has passed from the outbreak of the storm which is immediately over, as if it were a game. Alice seems to have stopped worrying.

That evening Nicholas crosses himself for all the company before they start eating, and again, as soon as he has finished the sacred gesture, the rain begins to roar down. They all serve themselves in silence, but restless eyes turn to the windows being pelted by volleys of muddy, reddish water.

—What do you think of this rain, Father?—

—It's very violent, Aleksei, as are many summer storms. I've never seen such sudden but brief ones: it's probably the area, the climate.—

—There is a hemorrhage in heaven; that water was stolen by Tatiana.—

Nicholas said nothing, looking at Alice, who was astonished and incapable of grasping what her son was saying. He understood, though, and that night he was awake for a long time, while crickets sang as they had done every night, and the air was so calm and muggy it was as if the daytime storm had been a dream. There was a perfect half-moon; it looked as if it had been drawn by Anastasia for one of Aleksei's books. The nightingale had taken up its song again, but it was a different tune, a more sorrowful one, with one long trembling note held at the end of each solo, before falling silent, as if anxious for a reply. Nicholas knew he should listen, but something was distracting him, something linked to the river, the crickets, the fireflies, to the moon in the sky. Life called him; it was difficult, so difficult not to feel the torment of leaving it, life was still beautiful even behind the prison glass, and he was ashamed not to be able to listen to what precious things the nightingale was singing to him.

—But I have no more time, no more strength to understand how I can save them. I cannot listen to you anymore.— And Nicholas looked at his ring in the reflection of the moonlight, the sapphire ring that had belonged to his father, which he could no longer remove from his finger.

—Listen, I crossed the whole of Siberia to come to you, don't waste time,— implored the nightingale; —you must beware of someone who is already here, you must beware, listen, Nicholas, listen . . .— the piteous nightingale insisted.

In the distance the Iset had slowed down, holding the breath of its current so as not to interrupt what the Tsar and the nightingale were saying to each other. Jurovsky slept in his room on the ground floor, after the decision taken the evening before by the Soviet, in the Hotel Amerika. The loss of water from the sky had to be repaired and there were various ways of doing it. History itself had taken a hand in it this time, having given carte blanche for the fate of the Romanovs in a telegram from the Moscow to the Ural Soviet. In Jurovsky's pocket were the pieces of paper on which the Bolsheviks had written the names of the eleven prisoners in Ipatiev's

house, voting their death sentence: in their mercy they had
spared Kharitonov's young scullery boy, Leonid.

The Whites were drawing near with the same slowness as
the one Nicholas could see reflected in the mirrors. Perhaps
both would come too late, and Nicholas and the river would
reach the sea with no more delays. Finally he knew what there
was to do, and he did not hesitate. He fixed his eyes to the
eyes in the mirror; with a desperate effort he managed not to
lower his gaze; he succeeded in maintaining his ground in that
battle with the devices in the mirror. And the Other appeared,
with that look, with those eyes that had seen death coming in
the Yussoupov palace in St. Petersburg.

—Go away, let us die in peace.—

—Without my help you will not be able to save your-
selves.—

—Go away and leave my daughter alone. We have no need
of you.—

—I can make your enemies die; you are a tsar and you
don't wish to be victorious?— Rasputin trembled, consumed
in an ever-dwindling flame. —I can give you power over time,
you can return to whatever year of your reign you wish, even
to your father's days, you can call him to your help with all
your brothers and their armies ... look carefully. ...—

And Nicholas saw in the mirror his brothers, first the
faded, pale image of George, then the prostrate image of Mikhail, and finally he recognized his father, saw his hands
stretched out that Nicholas might free them all from eternity.
But Nicholas hit the mirror with his fist: the house shook
lightly, he heard Aleksei's spaniel yelp and no one awoke.

Shaking, bathed in sweat, he faced the mirror once more:
only a crack had snapped its enchantment, but Nicholas saw

his face as he had never seen it. He had to lean against something, dizzy as he was with images: Mathilde, Alice, Elizabeth, his mother, the crowds in front of the Winter Palace, lastly an image that tormented him, a group of dispersed soldiers marching in Siberia with a torn Imperial flag and the voice of the commander losing itself in the wind before his fall from the horse, hit by a revolver shot. Who is this colonel? Nicholas recognizes him, knows that long face, has already seen those eyes, that look, so like a warning that has by now become useless. . . .

19

The jugglers and the acrobats who came to Tobolsk every year a few days before July 17, the feast day of their patron saint Aleksei, saw immediately how much it had changed. They came on high wagons that kept the secret of their marvels, every year different and every year the same. The first night they always spent at the Convent of St. Andrew where Vladimir's sister was a nun in a strictly enclosed order. Vladimir was blind in one eye, had pitch-black hair gathered in a braid and a single gold earring. Every year he would make sure all the instruments of conjuring were blessed: the machine that reproduced the sound of thunder, the one to make rain fall on the front rows of spectators, the masks, the distorting mirrors that reduced people until they almost disappeared, the explosive mixtures, the braziers with narcotic perfumes, the philters, the elixirs. Above all, he made sure Nana was blessed, the Tatar dwarf who had not stopped talking for 428 days, not even in her sleep. She announced this record herself, before the crowds started hissing and booing when the illusion of Atanor the Frenchman, the terrifying vision of flames on the city that should have sent the whole audience into a panic within five minutes, failed within three seconds, leaving a mild scent of lilac behind. Vladimir caught something from that insistent high-pitched voice that spewed a torrent of words:

—There is something wrong in the air! Everything is too slow, time has expanded, doubled its length for every trick. . . .—

Vladimir had to recognize that the dwarf, like all those cramped into a body too small for their minds, had sensed something very true: it was sufficient to repeat the trick, as he was doing, doubling the times of the magic formula and the enchantment was perfect again. But the people had waited long enough, there were rumblings in the square, some were already asking for their rubles back.

—Your ruble? But which one, my good people? There is no longer a tsar on your coins, how can we give you back what no longer belongs to you?— The devil take that dwarf, once again she had said too much. Vladimir hadn't even time to shut her mouth: she wanted to ruin them, talking of the Tsar on the coins in Tobolsk! How could she not know he had been a prisoner here for eight months and then they had taken him off? There must be no provocation about all that, it was dangerous; there might be a commissar of the people in the crowd. And why on earth was that ass Atanor coming in dressed like Nero? . . . Nothing was going right this morning. . . .

But looking at the crowd from the stage it seemed as if everyone had suddenly become distracted by something that was making them forget their disappointment over the failure of the Frenchman's act. People from various corners of the square raised their voices:

—It's true! The dwarf is right. Look, my rubles don't have the head of the Tsar!—

—Nor mine! Look.—

—It's true! There is only the year and the value.—

—How is it possible? Who's played this trick on us?—

Vladimir thought he would seize the opportunity, not knowing, just as the people of Tobolsk did not know, that those were the first coins of the Soviet government to reach them after the winter. These headless rubles would be his masterpiece of illusion, they would make up for the failed illusion; he was about to proclaim that this prodigy was the result of his magic when he felt a tug on his sleeve and the dwarf whispered to him not even to think of it, to drive it right out of his head, that it was dangerous to take on the responsibility for that face on the coins in a strange town like this. . . . It was true, Tobolsk had always been different from the other towns in Siberia; it was better not to joke with people like these . . . there was some evil among them; it was perhaps just as well if they made off earlier than on previous years. . . . The Siamese twins came onstage for their act, but few took any notice, still absorbed as they were by the rubles in their hands, that were worthless without the head of the Tsar. So it was true that at St. Petersburg there had been a revolution, that the Tsar was no longer the Tsar.

One August day they had seen him arrive with a retinue of 320 people, to go and stay at the governor's palace. Many houses had been requisitioned to make room for all his courtiers: ten ladies-in-waiting, twelve gentlemen-in-waiting, six chambermaids and two waiters, ten valets, three cooks, four scullery boys, a butler, a cellarer, a nurse, a clerk, a barber, three spaniels. And the 200 guards of Colonel Kobylinsky.

They said he was a prisoner, that there had been a revolution at St. Petersburg, but they hadn't really believed it: they saw their Tsar every day, walking in the town at the same hour in the afternoon, smiling, accompanied by the grand duchesses and his courtiers, while the guards could barely hold back the crowds who wanted to kiss his hand. It was well-known that the Tsaritsa never left the governor's palace, in order not to be separated from her son who was hemophiliac. But then other things must have happened in St. Petersburg; different soldiers had come to get him, Red soldiers, and the Tsar had gone away in April, with a smaller retinue, however, perhaps so that he could reach his palace at Tsarskoe Selo more quickly. But it was rumored that he had been stopped at Ekaterinburg. And in fact from the day he left they had felt bereft until a whole regiment of Red soldiers had arrived. Their commander, commissar of the people Nykolsky, had declared that there were no longer any noblemen, nor any tsar in the whole of Russia, that the war was over and soon the land would be given to the peasants. The town did not know what to believe. Since then too many things had begun to change and life had no longer been the same. The first novelty was the abolition of the "run of shame": for centuries the whores, Jews, three or four usurers, any beggars, some madmen, the dwarfs, had to compete in a race in Saint Aleksei Square, the women with no garment under their raised skirts, the men shaved and clothed in sackcloth like penitents. Then the Orlov fortress was emptied of the exiles: prisoners of state, even those guilty of assassination attempts on the Tsar's grandfather, were seen staggering from the doorway of the fortress, rubbing their eyes and lowering them quickly against the sun, blinded by the light they had not thought they would ever see again. The women ran away blessing themselves when the giant Colonel Ruzsky appeared, the terrorist who was the father of a great friend of the Tsar, a man so tall and large they had not been able to put him in a regulation cell, they had had to put him in the corner tower, from where every morning at the barred window he told the children his story, so that they would never leave Tobolsk, so that they would not repeat the mistake he had made as a boy, to run away stowed in the cart of the Jewish merchant from his village, to go down there, to St. Petersburg. . . .

After that, the storyteller was silenced, the man who beat his drums at sunset along the streets that were dusty in summer and icy in winter, telling tales of what might be happening in Moscow or St. Petersburg, as workers returned home from their day's labor, willing to dawdle and listen to distant, improbable tales. The new government, whose commissar lived now in the governor's palace and had barricaded himself in the center of his regiment, wanted the people to listen to the radio that had been placed in the marketplace, and to read the newspapers, not to listen to those lying old men, the storytellers.

It was that maniac of the commissar who stopped the clock in the tower of Saint Salvatore, the only clock in town, a gift from Tsaritsa Elizaveta, with its heavy white marble calendar which for almost two hundred years had displayed the days and the months of the Russian year—thirteen days behind the rest of the world. Armenians belonging to the Agagianian family were in charge of shifting the date by hand, while the old clock mechanism pushed the minutes forward. It was necessary that the citizens learn to be more precise, carry a watch, without depending on the delays of that absentminded family who frequently, especially in winter when time in Siberia stands still, forgot the minutes, the half hours, sometimes even the days.

After so many novelties, after such frequent and abrupt changes in their habits, after such series of strange and contradictory news about what was happening in the world, it was understandable that the crowd, eager for entertainment in the square in front of the conjurers' platform on the vigil of Saint Aleksei, had been irritated by the joke of the rubles: Vladimir had scarcely managed to take shelter in the wings before a shower of stone and coins hit the stage. Only later did the crowd begin to understand that Vladimir and his troupe were not to blame, and those coins were valid tender, were worth something, the kopecks and rubles of the new government.

Yes, Tobolsk was like a sick woman who could only find relief from her pain in her own bed, free of the duty of getting up and going to the doctor. All the town wanted was to return to the quietness it had always lived in, its spring market, its feast days for the Redeemer and for the harvest, its customs sanctified by the centuries. Why did they not let it drift on through the centuries, why wake it from its sleep, why bring to it an imprisoned Tsar, a regiment of Red soldiers, a new Soviet commissar?

Since the telegraph had started working again in April after the Tsar had left, the news that had flooded in was even stranger. Like the extraordinary news about the Preobrazhenskii Regiment, the regiment of Peter the Great, under the command of Prince Ypsilanti, marching through Siberia to reach Tobolsk. Would they not be happier without telegraph and radio, without the newspaper, sheets soiled by lead, that, however late, tried to reach them even here? Luckily it became clear that the news of the Preobrazhenskii had to be false: now, so many months later, there was no danger of it turning up from the plains. But the novelties never stopped.

One day the Soviet commissar, after closing down some churches that had been abandoned and returning the keys to the bishop, made a tour with a hundred soldiers to reconnoiter the convents of the town, to make a tally of the enclosed nuns still behind those walls: no one knew how many there were, not even old Bishop Hermogenes, who was ninety-seven and had stopped carrying out his duties some years before, even before he went blind. The people, shocked at this sacrilege, shut themselves up in their houses to avoid hearing the cries of the nuns forced by the soldiers to come out of the cells where they had hidden. Their number seemed so high to the commissar that he ordered half of them to go home. The bishop himself had been worried, in his time, by this phenomenal growth of the enclosed orders: it seemed ridiculous that he should have to close down churches for lack of priests, only to be put under pressure by the constant growth in the population of barren virgins who kept asking him for new confessors. He had frequently told them, during his last visits, when he could still see them all gathered around his bishop's chair in the choir, that it was not always true that God could be best served in silence and in the renunciation of family duties. But that someone would dare to violate the pact between God and those souls, that, Hermogenes could never approve, and it led him to regret even more the incomprehensible delay of the Holy Synod in Moscow, which for years had been hesitating about sending a new, young successor. He told all who came to visit him how much he was suffering from the indifference of the citizens over what had happened to the sisters in the convents.

But the immured women of Tobolsk, the nuns torn away from the cloistered life by the brute force of revolutionary troops, found a way to revenge themselves for the insults they had suffered and shake the town out of its indifference. They knew their fellow citizens well, their sisters, brothers, fathers, cousins, for whom they had prayed all their lives. They had been the depositories of the most intimate confessions and confidences, the outbursts and the bitterness on so many occasions. They well knew what a sense of guilt there was in the homes they had been forced to return to after so many years, over their families' cowardice displayed in front of the commissar of the people. One of them, Sister Pulcheria, Vladimir's sister, who had been abbess a few times, went to Vladimir the night after the sacrilegious act. He had taken refuge in an inn on the outskirts of Tobolsk, and was about to leave the town that had been so unwelcoming. They had an intense conversation lasting two hours and immediately afterward Vladimir closeted himself with Atanor, Solange, Nadia and all the other actors and acrobats in his troupe.

Two nights later the inhabitants of Tobolsk were terrified by voices from the dead: their dear ones threatened them with the most horrible misfortunes because of what they had let happen in their town. Everyone trembled, not daring to go out into the street. Everyone recognized the voice of their mother, father or brother, with just a touch of feminine sweetness to it: the nuns had listened for two days without a break to Vladimir and his friends, who, in the deconsecrated churches to which the bishop had given them the keys, surpassed themselves in teaching the pious virgins to modulate their voices until they could bring out sounds of resentment and reproach to perfection, while their memories helped them to recapture the voices of their dear ones, who had been dead for years but not forgotten. The storyteller, after thirty years of announcements, knew on which corner of what street his baritone voice would reverberate to the best advantage, became Bishop Cyril, the best loved of the dead pastors, the immediate predecessor to Hermogenes. All the old people recognized the voice as he led some hundreds of women through the town they were seeing for the first time, though they had always prayed for it.

The Agagianians, the family who from the tower of Saint Salvatore had for two hundred years helped the flow of time even in this town where it seemed a greater effort than anywhere else, were the link between the companies of fast-moving ghosts. The greatest shudders were provoked by the screams of the ex-prisoners of state, whom Vladimir had intercepted in the taverns where he'd seen them nodding off with boredom despite the vodka, and whom he had convinced to perform. They took part with enthusiasm, with an eagerness to revenge themselves against the town where the capacity to live without being aware of the passage of time was enacted most fully. In the role of those saints whom the citizens venerated in the twenty churches remaining open, and whose relics were the object of a cult that time had only consolidated, the former exiles became terrible avengers, hammering on doors, requiring a reason for the ingratitude of souls on whom so much grace had been heaped.

Ruzsky, the giant who had frightened the women when they had seen him drawn up to his full height in the doorway of the fortress, was the most effective of all the ex-convicts that night of holy terror, according to Sister Pulcheria. The nuns, forced, as a result of a sacrilege such as had not been seen since the days of the Tatars, to defend their rights by raising the dead, followed him, as he threatened anathema along the streets, with greater intensity than they had ever followed any sermon by the bishop on his pastoral visits.

The next day the town was as quiet as a grave. Only the Red guards and the commissar wandered the city trying to track down the subversives who had vanished into the night like ghosts. Behind the doors of the twenty churches the nuns listened, with the help of the priests summoned with all speed by the bishop who had yielded without difficulties to Sister Pulcheria's entreaties the day before. For a few days Tobolsk seemed incapable of resuming its normal life, and the Red guards decided wisely not to try to make any contact with a bristly and sullen people, who were perplexed and did not know how to react to the latest upsets. But when some Jewish merchants arrived all breathless in the market square, wild-eyed and tripping over their long caftans, to announce that the Preobrazhenskii Regiment was on its way up from the river, the crowd knew what to do at once.

From every road, from every dusty street, from the square full of animals and merchants, from the shops, the government offices, the taverns and the churches, a general revolt sprang up. Everything was used to drive the soldiers of the new government from the town: scythes, axes, stones, tiles, sticks, pitchforks, old rifles, slings, metal bars, flagpoles, picks. Even the nuns from the desecrated convents took part in the spontaneous rebellion, the people noticed with admiration: they rushed against the Red soldiers as if they had always known fighting in the streets.

When, toward evening, they saw that their town was free and Bishop Hermogenes, in the cope and crown worn by his venerable predecessors, was lifted and carried by Vladimir and Pulcheria to appear, looking moved, in the doorway of his modest palace to bless the people of Tobolsk and welcome the most glorious regiment of the Tsar of all the Russias, to whose invincible commander he would give the keys of the town of Saint Aleksei, the whole crowd thought they were living a diabolical dream when they saw in front of them some fifty frightened and exhausted soldiers, blank-faced, as if they had come from a country where there was nothing new left to be seen, and some officers in rags, completely exhausted—a group of wretches without a leader, Prince Ypsilanti having shot himself with his revolver on sight of the rounded bell towers of the town.

20

On the morning of Monday, the sixteenth of July 1918, in Ipatiev's house, thousands of versts from restless Tobolsk, the Tsar still slept, though all his family was awake.

—Nicholas, Nicholas, wake up, we've already had breakfast without you, it's nine o'clock, my dear. . . .—

Where was he? Slowly the outline of the face of an old woman bent over him appeared in front of his eyes, then the dirty windows of a room, a half-opened door off its hinges, an iron bedstead. Was he at Tobolsk? No, it was not Tobolsk. It must be Tsarskoe Selo, because in the nearby woods birds were singing. But what was that soldier doing, standing in the half-open doorway?

—Aleksei's temperature has dropped, the doctor says he's over the crisis.— It was Alice, his wife, and he was a prisoner in Ekaterinburg with all his children.

—I'm sorry I slept so long.—

—Tatiana is not well.— The words spoken by Alice as he pulled himself up to sit in bed startled him, but he did not show it and left the mother to look after his daughter. He could still see the face of the commander lost with his soldiers

in the Siberian plains, that looked like a stifled shout: who was
he? Aleksei had come back into the room to play and seemed
to pay no attention to a phenomenon that surprised all the
others: the birds that morning had been visibly increasing in
number for some hours. The blackbirds, with their sharp
whistles, seemed to have taken over the higher part of the
roof. Some turtledoves were just then circling the house, looking for space to alight. Titmice had settled with the blackcaps
on the shutters, and framed the windows with their wings. The
Tsarevich, who must have predicted it and did not even talk
of it, was glancing through a fairy tale book, a gift from Pro-
fessor Gilliard for his last birthday. There was a brief history
of the origins of Russia, which the Swiss tutor had often explained to his pupil.

—I'd like to go here, Father,— and he pointed in his book
to a map of the world in which America did not yet feature,
and he indicated little Iceland, there out on the edge of the
world: four cartouches showed at the corners the swollen
cheeks of the wind, the golden chariot of the sun, night sleeping on the clouds, the naked sea-god on his shell. But the
small island, with its peninsula like a goose's claws, stretching
out to the west, seemed to run off the map of the world, as
though respecting that it was not quite complete.

—How big Russia is, look, Father, look.— Tsar and Tsarevich looked at the ancient map, at the space occupied by the
Russian Empire, so big that Europe was not equal to even half
of the half of it.

The golden domes of the Kremlin were there, at the heart
of it, near the palace where Aleksei would get lost even when
his mother was only four rooms away.

—Tomorrow is Saint Aleksei's Day, and in a few days it's

your birthday. You must forget you've been ill; to get well it's important not to think of the illness. Fourteen years are many, Aleksei: I was already a prisoner at fourteen, although not in the way you are. . . .—

—Prisoner, Father?—

—I wasn't free even if I did have freedom. The entire day was mapped out by those responsible for my education. When we get back home, you'll see what I mean, the Tsarevich is never free.—

—I don't want to be old, but if I have to, I'd like to be like you when I am!— Nicholas looked at his son tenderly: even though he was ill, even though he was no longer heir to the throne, to any throne, he too would have the right to enter the memory of mankind with his father and with all the monarchs Russia had produced.

From the moment when the evil forces had left Ipatiev's house, Nicholas began to think as if he had already lived out his life, looking back on it and on that of his family as one looks back on what is ended and accomplished. He was and always would be Nicholas II, Tsar of Holy Russia, and his son, Tsarevich Aleksei, would forever be heir. Forever. The revolution could not erase it. He and his children would live that kind of immortality. Nicholas was thinking of the millions of lives that disappeared as if they had never existed, of those secret treasures not enjoyed by anyone. He looked at his patched and threadbare trousers, looked at the cloth that could not last much longer, and thought of the photographs the soldiers had been taking over the last year and a half: the former Tsar working in the garden with his children, the former Tsarevich walking with Nagorny the sailor. He had never liked being photographed, but he could not even look at these.

Perhaps they would be used soon to remember his family. He felt as if his gaze, fixed to the lens of the camera, started a journey from which there was no possible return. He would never look at these photos as an album is looked at, taking pleasure in the years that pass and never stop; those images would never return to be juxtaposed to the bodies shown. They were photographic studies for a princely burial. The power wielded for twenty-two years was fixed in those snapshots so that the limits of the period should be respected. Nicholas practiced living in those images of himself hung on walls of houses he would never see, between the pages of books where the history of those days would be falsified day by day. He began to think of those strangers who would come there to see the house, and he was taken with nausea for history and a powerful envy for lives that left neither name nor memory behind them, that did not even leave a gravestone. He would have liked to die completely, for all eternity, with his companion the body.

But these were only momentary feelings, before he was taken again with profound pity for Aleksei and his daughters, a pity soothed only by the knowledge of a new awakening.

—Can you hear, Father? Someone is crying in there.— It was true; in the room next door one of his daughters was crying, and he knew which one.

Kharitonov the cook, meanwhile, was singing in the kitchen: a strange cheerfulness seeing that he could no longer do his own cooking, that food came ready from the same kitchen as the soldiers', and all he did was to warm up the soups and the roasts, though with the same love as always. Ah, to be still in Tsarskoe Selo, in front of the stove, able to invent the most exquisite variations on the Russian dishes, for all the kings that came to visit the Tsar! Now, in front of all the empty saucepans, reduced merely to preparing breakfast coffee, Kharitonov spent his days polishing his useless utensils and remembering the banquets of the most sumptuous court of Europe. But that day those saucepans that had justified his whole life had been called back into use: Jurovsky had had fifty eggs brought from one of the convents in the town for the prisoners, and had even remembered a skein of red wool that one of the grand duchesses had requested for an embroidery. Kharitonov decided to use some of those eggs to make a nice cake and had started to work on it secretly, to give the Tsarevich a great surprise: the next day was his name day and in two weeks it would be his birthday, and who knows whether they would be getting any more eggs by then? That 30th of July, the day of the Tsarevich's birth, seemed never to come any closer, the days were so identical. For the Tsar's and the Tsaritsa's birthdays in May and June they hadn't even been able to toast their health with a decent wine, the cook thought as he worked cheerfully. At least this time he would have to do something special, seeing he had so many eggs; and Kharitonov sang, sang that morning of the sixteenth of July 1918, as if he had returned to the kitchen of the Alexander Palace in Tsarskoe Selo and were preparing breakfast for the Tsar's guest, the Shah of Persia.

Alice, coming out of the grand duchesses' room, whispered to Nicholas that Tatiana was delirious: the doctor reckoned that it was something she had eaten. Nicholas said nothing, happy that Alice should feel stronger that day: she seemed well able to stand, and Aleksei could take a few steps. There was such a strong bond between mother and son that Aleksei could pass on to her any improvements he felt himself. How she had aged. The times when she had vied with Maman, the young widow of Alexander III, to lend the monarchy the charm of feminine beauty . . . waking that morning he had thought she was a stranger. Yet now she too is different from usual, Nicholas told himself; she moves as she used to the times when we were leaving the next day and she had a thousand orders to give.

—Look, Father, what funny soldiers!— Aleksei called to him as he turned the pages of his book. He showed him a reproduction of a painting from Paris by an Italian. The artist had illustrated it with a battle between Trojans and Greeks under the walls of Troy. They were clearly Renaissance costumes and Aleksei, even though he did not know these historic differences, looked on enchanted at the horsemen in the middle of the dogs and leverets, thinking how different they were from the horsemen he imagined in the *Iliad*.

—Now painters don't depict soldiers anymore; there are photographs instead. Do you remember those in the regiments at Stavka, Aleksei?—

—But are these photographs of the Preobrazhenskii Regiment? And of Prince Ypsilanti too?—

At this, the face that had been haunting him for days rose to Nicholas's mind: it was he, Ypsilanti, most definitely the commander of the Preobrazhenskii. His was the long face, the wild look, it was he at the head of a haggard squad of the lost. . . .

—No, those in the Preobrazhenskii Regiment don't get photographed by anyone, only a painter has represented them; the painting is in my study in Petrograd. . . .—

—Father, you don't like photographs, but this one is beautiful.— And Aleksei showed his father the one of the princely couple from Kiev in their monuments. They had died in their youth and slept in their wedding clothes, she in a long peplum with a fur cap, he in his armor with the visor open.

Nicholas took the book and had a better look at them. He knew their story: they had died three centuries before, at eighteen, the very day of their wedding, and the town had commemorated their death in a splendid monument to life. To Nicholas their faces seemed so weighted down with thoughts as to leave no second of doubt that they would never wake again, lying there dead in the full bloom of their youth. They were different, their thoughts, from those of someone asleep: and to reach their thoughts, Nicholas had a great wish to abandon the ones he had. Someone must have led the artist to the place where the two young people had woken. Her lips were more tightly shut, convinced she should keep what she saw to herself; the warrior was the one more tempted to confide something, with his lips slightly parted as if he were still breathing, barely showing small teeth. But it was the eyelids, completely relaxed, that intimated the invincible strength that comes from death: the seductiveness of those lids distracted the onlooker from listening to what the lips might have to say, for fear that they would deny the happiness of the vision. But she, she seemed to have forgotten life, to be satisfied, full of the sweetness of death.

—Do they frighten you, those photographs?— Aleksei watched his father with a mischievous smile, hourly less predictable, less of a child. —They're so beautiful it's difficult to remember they're dead, don't you think? They're not even frightening. But I wouldn't want to be the sculptor who carved them. Look, look, more birds are coming, Father, look. Where are they going to find a perch?—

Nicholas turned, drew near the window and recognized the newcomers, all on the electric-light wires.

—I wonder where they come from? I would so like to fly. You, you know what it feels like, you did up there on the balcony of the palace when you declared war on Germany. I was ill, remember, I wasn't in uniform, standing with you on the balcony. Flying must be like being in charge of a regiment. . . .—

And Nicholas, turning to look at his son, saw in his eyes a trace of resentment, as if he had been deprived of the pleasure of flight. But Aleksei was only pretending not to know where those birds came from that landed in waves, not to upset his father. He in fact knew their origin, their names, the reasons for their loyalty, the price they had paid for such a painful metamorphosis. He knew that before they had become birds, landing in flocks on the roof of this house and recognizing each other after the brief separation, they had been soldiers of a whole regiment that had been undone during a long march through Siberia, a regiment that had lost contact with the rest of the world, had become a prisoner of the vastness, scattering itself partly in the taiga, partly on the plain in the futile search for their Tsar, to rescue him; they had been scattered, dispersed, lost through a tragic chain of misunderstandings, delays and revolts. Now that the last of them was reaching the roof of Ipatiev's house, having died from a terrible typhoid epidemic on the road to Tobolsk, along which the pitiful deceit of their commander had taken them to their death, as he looked for a last pretext to keep from them the truth of their fate, they seemed anxious not to miss the last appointment with all their comrades who had preceded them, dying of cold on the road to Vachitino. And Aleksei knew that soon, very soon, before another sunrise, all the inhabitants of that house, he, his parents, his sisters, the four faithful servants, one of the guards and those creatures outside the window, would take flight together.

Later Tatiana came out of her room, extremely pale, wearing a red silk kerchief to her neck which she knotted and unknotted constantly. With her forehead against the glass, that dirty glass that Jurovsky had partly daubed with white paint that morning to prevent the prisoners from seeing out, she seemed to be looking out intently, undaunted by the white, or by the tall fence around the house. She felt that Rasputin had really abandoned them this time, and her father had won. She was worried in case some word had escaped her during her delirium, that her mother and sisters may have heard. She knew her father had understood and dreaded the moment when he would address her. How she hated him at times! Men on the Russian throne had not always been exemplary, but the women had always distinguished themselves. She would have reigned like the great Catherine, without the scruples of her indecisive father, so concerned with the religious conscience of the people. She opened the golden medallion with the miniature of Catherine II and of Grandmother Maria Feodorovna that she wore as a necklace: she looked at the strong hands, the knotted arthritic fingers, the narrow, small nails. The miniaturist had carefully observed those hands, the hands of the most atheist sovereign in Europe, hands which so greatly resembled hers, she thought, as she closed the medallion and returned to her sisters' room to sit and read, taking advantage of their absence. She suffered from the lack of space; she found the constant proximity of her family oppressive. In their places of confinement she had always looked for a protective strength in the cherished objects she had managed to bring with her from Tsarskoe Selo and was irritated when her sisters did not understand her need to arrange them in order at once, wherever they happened to be. She knew objects had a value well beyond the value of their usefulness and she had learned to be humble with them, she knew how to listen to them. Tatiana's hands were immediately striking: nervous and changeable, they could become twisted into the sharpest spasm, and revert instantly into white, marmoreal stillness. She used them wonderfully to sew, to cook, to embroider and draw, all things she performed to perfection. Objects obeyed those hands.

Nicholas, coming into the room that moment looking for Alice, found his daughter alone, absorbed in a book. Tatiana lifted her head abruptly and blushed, but held her father's gaze.

—Tatiana, are you better?—

—Yes, as you can see.—

—I would like you to be more serene.—

They were silent for a few moments. Nicholas came near.

—Tatiana, you're not accepting death.—

—Certainly, I would do anything not to die. I love this body of mine, I don't understand your resignation.—

—You don't believe in anything but yourself, you're not willing to change form or place.—

—But death is flesh, brain, nerves, tendons that break, blood that is scattered everywhere, just like Kharitonov's chickens, when he cleans them and tears out liver and heart!—

—So you would move heaven and earth to save those fragments of flesh? And how would you conquer old age?—

—I don't want to know. While I have youth and beauty I don't think of death. While you, you've reigned in the service of death.—

—Do you think that these revolutionaries will wield power according to a love of this land like yours?—

—I don't know, they're so confused. For the moment they're only justified by having routed you.—

—Whatever you may believe, remember that I will never accept our salvation through the intervention of the one you have invoked. I continue to represent God even in Ipatiev's house, up to the moment of sacrifice, a sacrifice that will be mine. It is I who am the Tsar.—

—I've seen the mirror, you need not worry. He will not come again.—

Nicholas ran his fingers lightly through her fine blond hair and felt a profound anguish at the thought of that young body that wanted life, felt that young flesh, feared he would not be able to hold out against despair.

"Take courage, Nicholas, have the courage to be afraid." It was the voice already heard in the night, when he had no longer felt terror at plunging into the dark. Ah, if only Tatiana could have heard that voice! But it spoke only to one at a time. He left the room as the sisters came in.

—Aleksei is better, look, he's talking to Jurovsky. . . .—

And so it was, the commander of the guards sat close to Aleksei's wheelchair, talking to Alice. He had never before sat with his prisoners, but had always remained standing, delivering his dry abrupt orders; now he rose as Nicholas came in.

—Your son is better today.—

—We thank you for the eggs.—

Nicholas had to stand there, smiling, next to his executioner, as if he were still Tsar, as if the other were one of his many subordinates. On the edge of the abyss, he had to play his own part with grace, to pretend he had had enough to spare, that he could leave this life behind, as if he could give more but had no wish to do so. He did not manage his part, though, and took Aleksei back to his room. Jurovsky left immediately. It's too much that you should come and play with your victims, Nicholas thought, remembering Kobylinsky, the loyal colonel who had brought them from Tsarskoe Selo to Tobolsk, who had knelt in front of them when he had had to leave them for their journey to Ekaterinburg. Tomorrow, who would come? Who would succeed Jurovsky? While these thoughts raced through his mind, he looked through the upper part of the window at a white kaolin cup, the kind that is attached to light poles to separate the wires and hold them suspended between one pole and the next. He would have liked never to have been born, to have inhabited any body but the body of Nicholas II. He envied the white cup fixed to the pole, that lifeless object, and he immersed himself completely in the shape of that little inverted cup from which no one might drink. The peace of that fragment of kaolin, its nullity, its being just one of an identical series of millions of cups that sustained the light on the poles of the vastest empire in the world . . . why be born son of a tsar and not kaolin in a seam of mineral inside a mountain? Why be anything rather than just nothing? He expiated day by day the centuries through which the Russian monarchy had labored to construct its image. He took a magnifying glass and looked at the palm of his hand, then at the back of it. He was that thing with those red and pink wrinkles, the parallel lines, the long black hairs, the small craters, the blemishes, the blue welts. What landscape was this? A valley inhabited years and years before. The last ones had left, abandoning the vegetation to itself; the stems of reeds had grown so long they hid the way. And the wells? Or had it been stars, meteors, that had furrowed the earth thus, to leave these craters? The sun must have ravaged the valley; yet one time it had been so full of life. . . .

—Father, what are you doing? It looks as if you want to see your blood. . . .—

Aleksei had come in silently and surprised him.

—Let's see if our hands are similar, come here.— Aleksei pushed his wheelchair close to his father. Nicholas took his son's hands, joined them together and took them to his own eyes, then to his lips to kiss them.

—Are you all right, Father?—

—What was that man saying to you?—

—He was talking to Mother, not me.—

—Didn't you hear anything?—

—No, I was listening to the soldiers who were singing downstairs. Listen to them, they're still singing . . . it's not a horrible song, it's one that talks of a girl who waits for her soldier to come back to the village and he returns after many years. . . .—

—And how does it end?—

—The soldier returns, but the girl has gone and so he looks for her, he searches and doesn't find her. . .—

—Why are you stopping? Go on.—

—So one day the soldier comes to you–anyway, goes to the Tsar and asks him to help find his girl, to send out his cossacks to look until they find her.—

—Then what do I do?—

—You put on the soldier's clothes, and dress the soldier as

Tsar. You tell him to wait, that you will soon return with the girl . . .— Aleksei didn't go on; he stopped and stared at his father.

—And then?—

—Then, then, then you came in and I couldn't hear, and now they're singing, but you wanted to know the song so we'll never know the end.—

Aleksei went to the window to listen, but the singing had stopped and the soldiers had gone in. The boy seemed so disappointed at the silence that Nicholas pretended to know the song.

—It's an old song, I know it. I'll tell you how it ends; I was only asking to make sure it really was the one I know.—

Aleksei turned, absolutely attentive.

—I don't go back to the soldier in my palace; the soldier waits and plays Tsar in my place forever.—

—Do you not go back because you're still looking for the girl or because you don't want to be Tsar anymore?—

Nicholas saw the blue eyes of his son open wider than he had ever seen them before.

—The song doesn't say; it ends like this, at least in the version I know,— he answered smiling. Aleksei was still, thinking; slowly he began to hum the melody, until Kharitonov came to announce that lunch was ready.

Everyone was already at table: Alice, with Olga and Maria on either side of her, then Tatiana, Anastasia, the Tsar's and the Tsarevich's empty places, then the doctor and the three guards on duty. Trup and Demidova were serving, with the help of the cook. Nicholas, before sitting, placed the wheelchair, made a sign of the cross and said grace aloud. Aleksei noticed the absence of Leonid, the little scullery boy. Jurovsky had told him that he was no longer needed, he was now to stay home with his friends the Popovs; he could take the Tsarevich's chair, the one on castors that he liked so much, and he could play with it if he wanted—the Tsarevich had another one. The soldiers, in silence, had already begun to eat. Nicholas was not to know that in the Caucasus from where they came, those soldiers had buried courtiers alive with their own hands: Prince Ourousov, the old secretary to his brother George, and the prince's son, childhood friend of Aleksei and a member of the Imperial corps of pages.

The conversation was unusually lively. The doctor was telling the Tsaritsa about his children, left in Berlin, from whom he'd received good news that morning; the Tsaritsa listened carefully, serving her son. The Tsar, looking sideways at Tatiana, who was talking with Olga, spoke in French to Anastasia. Maria interrupted Tatiana to turn to whisper something to Olga and burst out laughing, glancing to the end of the table at the soldiers. Demidova, more excited and jocular than usual, changed the plates even before they were ready, and every once in a while went into the kitchen to consult the cook, sending the valet away.

—Off you go, see to the soldiers,— she said, laughing. Everyone was expecting Kharitonov's great cake, but in order not to mar the cook's pleasure, or Aleksei's love of surprises—and he had a passion for desserts—they all kept up the pretense of ignorance.

—Are we going to give some to those louts?— the Tsaritsa's maid asked the cook, who shrugged as if to say, "We can't very well not give them any, can we? You know that." The doctor started a discussion with the Tsar on the behavior of the French troops in war. He knew the Tsar had a liking for the French and that he had felt particularly betrayed after the revolution when he had read the commentaries in the foreign papers about his fall. So many years of secure alliance, such steadfastness on the part of his army in keeping the Germans occupied at the time of the Marne, to avoid the fall of Paris, and then so much scorn and so many accusations. The doctor, taking advantage of Nicholas's greater talkativeness, wanted the Tsar to admit the superiority of the Russian courage over that of the French, whose soldiers were easily discouraged, emotional, incapable of group discipline. It was not that the Tsar disagreed, but a growing unease prevented him from continuing the discussion. He would have given half his former powers to know from those three soldiers who ate in silence what they thought of the Russian and the French fighting men. He looked at them often: he knew they were part of the team of ten Letts in the secret police, sent a few days before to take over duties at "the house of special designation." He did not think they were all Letts, as the less-educated Russians called the non-Russian speakers of the empire. Perhaps one or two of them were Magyars, Austro-Hungarian prisoners of war. How much might they be able to tell Nicholas about the behavior of the Russian soldier. Nicholas would have liked to have been a foreign soldier, watching the imprisoned Imperial family at table.

Who were they, those three soldiers? Was the Tsaritsa so very different from their women? And the Tsar of Russia? Was their silence embarrassment or indifference? He was struck by their way of eating: slowly, carefully, methodically. They lifted their heads from the table only rarely, did not talk among themselves; they served themselves calmly and confidently, as if they might be in just any place where food is provided. They left nothing on their plates, but they ate with no appetite. He was fascinated by their hands, so hard and exact, so strong and silent. Nicholas felt suddenly ridiculous: they, the conversation with the doctor, all of them, were all ridiculous, absurd, faced with those soldiers. The sham gaiety of an ordinary July day in 1918, the usual titles, Your Imperial Majesty, Imperial Highness, the patriotic discussions, the French lesson, the cake by the court cook, in front of those three who cut their meat in complete silence.

Aleksei served himself slowly, still thinking of the song. If he had been Tsar he would have certainly found the girl, he would have looked for her with the soldiers. Why did the song say the Tsar went alone? Why dressed as an ordinary soldier? And why had he not come back? And the Tsarevich paused like that, his fork poised in midair, wondering how the soldiers' song ended; not the one his father had told him. Because his father had not sung it, he had simply recited it. But the soldiers were there now, in front of him; they were eating with them. How much he wanted to ask them to go on singing! But what would his mother say if he started talking to them? He tried catching their eye by staring at them; it was not easy because Tatiana was looking at him. There was one especially who seemed nice, the one in the middle, with a beard. He glanced at Aleksei for a moment. Kharitonov appeared triumphantly, carrying the large cake on a great cardboard tray. There was clapping, exclamations of surprise and approval as Trup and Demidova made room for it in the middle of the table. Aleksei is the first one to be served and Nicholas gives him permission to start immediately. Even Alice is smiling. Suddenly Aleksei stops eating and whispers to his father, asking his permission to offer a slice to the soldiers. Alice has not heard and leans toward Nicholas while Aleksei has already moved and stands, excited, next to the soldiers. He hands over the plate with three slices and asks the middle one if they were the ones singing that morning and if they could sing that song again, please. The three take the cake with the same silence with which they received the food from Trup and Demidova. The middle one with the beard gestures that he does not understand Russian, did not understand the question. Aleksei realizes that it could not have been them, they could not have been the soldiers who sang, and returns to his place. The cook meanwhile is being praised by everyone for the delicious cake and the conversation resumes, this time between Olga, Maria and Anastasia, a conversation about what gift to give the priest for his church when he next visits them, about Anastasia's drawing which the sisters would like to frame and hang on the bleak walls. Aleksei turns to look at the windows: he has heard the whir of wings, the last, the most faithful, the most tired have arrived. There is no room for more, the hour must be near. Tatiana draws close to him and gives him her piece of cake.

—Aleksei, it is too much for me,— and she passed her hand through his hair, smiling, and handed him the first barely ripe pomegranate from the tree.

—Anastasia said I should wait for your birthday, but I thought it would be nicer to give it to you today. The others have already tasted it and they say it's not completely ripe, but it's good. Do you see how the seeds are all packed so close?— And Tatiana's eyes, looking at her brother, filled with tears she could not hold back. Aleksei cut off another piece of the skin and gazed at the little red seeds held tightly together in the shell.

—Not one falls, there are so many, so many they can't be counted.— The Tsarevich had started to suck some of the seeds and looked at the fruit thinking he was not going to finish it.

Toward evening Aleksei fell asleep with the pomegranate still in his hand and Nicholas found him stretched across the bed. The father looked down at him, at the lengthening shadows: the days were shorter already, already there was an inkling of premature autumn. Aleksei was so beautiful, so relaxed, so tranquil in sleep after having played so long in the afternoon. The nightshirt, silk embroidered with red by his sister, was unbuttoned at the neck.

By evening my beard has grown black and hard, but your hair, like spun sugar, is quite undisturbed, not even the wind has ruffled it. Who are you? Nicholas asked himself, as he caressed his sleeping son. He delicately took the pomegranate from the boy's hand and tasted a seed. God was near him and everything was ready.

At midnight Jurovsky and his soldiers climbed the stairs, their rifles loaded and cocked. On the second floor they knocked at the prisoners' door, but there was no reply. They hurled the door down and saw, each in his or her bed, the bodies of those whom Tatiana had mercifully put to sleep forever with the poisoned fruit. The pomegranate lay there, in the center of the room where it had rolled after it had fallen from Tatiana's hand, for she, after her dear ones, had been the last to eat from it. A furious Jurovsky had no time to prevent the soldier Dimitri from sucking a few seeds, and watched him fall to the ground a few minutes later. At the sweet sound of the nightingale all the birds seemed to wake from the great aviary that Ipatiev's house had become and to launch themselves like the Furies against the Reds with their beaks, their claws, diving at the top of their heads, aiming for eyes, mouths, hands. And a wind from the east rose up that tore and uprooted the trees in the garden where Aleksei had so often played. The greenhouse, the fence with the sentry posts, the gates, the iron benches, the hedges of sycamore, the light poles, the tools used by Nicholas for cutting timber, all were swept away in the fury of that blast. The eagle reappeared, high above the tallest part of the house, hovered, and only Jurovsky, protecting his face from the last bird, saw it take charge of the winged regiment about to take flight. And while God took back the power lent to men who had not been able to understand it, the windows flew open that had been shut to prevent the Imperial family from seeing beyond the garden, to where the Whites were firing, as at that very moment they broke through into the city, to rescue, too late, the Tsar of all the Russias.

The text of this book was set in Cloister.

Composed by

Graphic Composition, Inc., Athens, Georgia.

Printed and bound by

The Haddon Craftsmen, Inc., Scranton, Pennsylvania.

Designed by Julie Duquet